THE MAN IN THE
WOODEN HAT

JANE GARDAM

ABACUS

First published in Great Britain in 2009 by Chatto & Windus
This paperback edition published in 2011 by Abacus
Reprinted 2011 (twice)

ISBN 978-0-349-11846-8

Typeset in Sabon by M Rules
Printed and bound in Great Britain by
Clays Ltd, St Ives plc

Abacus
An imprint of
Little, Brown Book Group
100 Victoria Embankment
London EC4Y 0DY

An Hachette UK Company
www.hachette.co.uk

www.littlebrown.co.uk

For David

Contents

PART ONE:
Marriage

Chapter One

There is a glorious part of England known as the Donheads. The Donheads are a tangle of villages loosely interlinked by winding lanes and identified by the names of saints. There is Donhead St Mary, Donhead St Andrew, Donhead St James and, among yet others, Donhead St Ague.

This communion of saints sometimes surprises new-comers if they are not religious and do not attach them to the names of village churches. Some do, for the old families here have a strong Roman Catholic tinge. It was Cavalier country. Outsiders, however, call the Donheads 'Thomas Hardy country', and it is so described by the estate agents who sell the old cottages of the poor to the rich.

And not entirely truthfully, for Hardy lived rather more to the south-west. The only poet celebrated for visiting a Donhead seems to be Samuel Taylor Coleridge, who came to see a local bookish bigwig but stayed for only one night. Perhaps it was the damp. The Donhead known as Ague seems connected to no saint and is thought to be a localised Bronze Age joke. Even so, it is the most desirable of all the villages, the most beautiful and certainly the most secluded, deep in miles of luxuriant woodland, its lanes thick with flowers. The small farms have all gone, and so have the busy village communities. The lanes are too narrow for the modern-day agricultural machinery that thunders through more open country. At weekends the rich come rolling down from London in huge cars full of provisions bought in metropolitan farmers' markets. These people make few friends in their second homes, unless they have connections to the great houses that still stand silent in their parks, still have a butler and are now owned by usually absent celebrities. There is a lack of any knockabout young.

Which makes the place attractive to the retired professional classes who had the wit to snap up a property years ago. Their children try not to show their anxiety that the agues of years will cause the old things to be taken into care homes and their houses to be pounced upon by the Inland Revenue.

In Donhead St Ague there is a rough earth slope, too countrified to be called a driveway, to the left of the village hill. Almost at once it divides into separate branches, one left, one right, one down, one up. At the end of the left-hand, down-sloping driveway stands the excellently modernised old farmhouse of Sir Edward Feathers QC (retired), who has lived there in peace for years. His wife Elisabeth – Betty – died while she was planting tulips against an old red wall. The house lies low, turned away from the village, towards the chalk line of the horizon and an ancient circle of trees on a hilltop. The right-hand driveway turns steeply upwards in

4

the other direction to be lost in pine trees. Round the corner, high above it, is a patch of yellow gravel and a house of ox-blood brick; apart from one impediment, it shares the same splendid view as Eddie Feathers's house below. The impediment is Feathers's great stone chimney that looks older than the house and has a star among the listed glories of the area. Maybe the house was once a bakery. The people in the ugly house above have to peep round the chimney to see the sunset.

There have been the same old local people in the ox-blood house, however, for years, and they are even-tempered. The house has become a sort of dower house for elderly members of a farming family who don't mix and, anyway, farmers seldom look at a view. They have never complained.

One day, however, they are gone. Vans and cars and 'family members' whisk them all away and leave Eddie Feathers to enjoy the view all by himself. He is rather huffed that none of them called to say goodbye, though for over twenty years he has never more than nodded to them in a chance encounter by the road. He wonders who will be his new neighbours. But not much.

The village wonders, too. Someone has seen the hideous house advertised for sale in *Country Life* at an astounding price, the photograph making it look like a fairy palace, with turrets. And no chimney in sight.

But nobody comes to visit it for some time. Down by the road a London firm of estate agents puts up a smart notice which Edward Feathers fumes about, not only because of the vulgarity of having to *advertise* a house in the Donheads,

5

especially in St Ague, but because someone might just possibly think that it referred to his.

Weeks and months passed. The right-hand driveway became overgrown with weeds. Somebody said they had seen something peculiar going on there one early morning. A dwarf standing in the lane. But nothing of any newcomer.

'A dwarf?'

'Well, that's what the paper boy said. Dropping in Sir Edward's paper down that bit of drainpipe. Seven in the morning. Mind, he's not what he was.' (The paper boy was seventy.)

'There are no dwarfs now. They've found a way of stopping it.'

'Well, it was a dwarf,' said the post boy. 'In a big hat.'

Chapter Two

Rather more than half a century earlier, when cows still came swinging up the Donhead lanes and chickens sat roosting in the middle of their roads, and there were blacksmiths, and the village shop was the centre of the universe, and most people had not been beyond Shaftesbury unless they'd been in the armed forces in the war, a young English girl was standing in the bedroom of a second-class Hong Kong hotel holding a letter against her face. 'Oh,' she was saying. 'Yes.'

'Oh, *yes*,' she told the letter. 'Oh, yes, I think so!' Her face was a great smile.

And at about the same moment, though of course it was yesterday for the Orient, an unusual pair was sitting in the glossy new airport for London (now called Heathrow) in England (now being called mysteriously the UK) waiting for a Hong Kong flight. One of the men, pretty near his prime, that's to say just over thirty, was English and very tall, and wore a slightly dated hand-made suit and shoes bought in Piccadilly (St James's Street). He was a man of unconscious distinction, and if he'd been wearing a hat you might think you were seeing a ghost. As it was, you felt he had been born to an earlier England.

His companion was a Chinese dwarf.

That at any rate was how he was described by the lawyers at the English Bar. The tall man was a barrister; a junior member of the Inner Temple and already spoken of with respect. The dwarf was a solicitor with an international reputation, only notionally Chinese. He preferred to be known as a Hakkar, the ancient red-brown tribe of oriental gypsies. He was treated with even greater respect than the barrister – who was, of course, Edward Feathers, soon to be known as 'Old Filth' (Filth an acronym for Failed in London Try Hong Kong) – for he held a gold mine of litigation at his disposal all over the world wherever English Law obtained. The dwarf could spot winners.

His name was Albert Loss. It was really Albert Ross, but the R was difficult for him to pronounce in his otherwise flawless English. This annoyed him, 'I am Loss' being not encouraging to clients. He claimed to have been at Eton but even to Feathers his origins were hazy. He worked the name Ross as near as possible to the Scottish nobility, and hinted at Glamis and deer-stalking in the glens. Sometimes he was jovially called 'Albatross', hence 'Coleridge' or 'Ancient Mariner', to which he responded with an inclination of the head. He was impossibly vain. To Eddie Feathers he had been, since the age of sixteen, a wonderful, if stern, friend.

Below the waist, hidden now by the table in the airport's first-class lounge at which he was playing a game of

8

Patience, Ross's sturdy torso dwindled down into poor little legs and block feet in Dr Scholl's orthopaedic sandals. The legs suggested an unfortunate birth and a rickety childhood. No one ever found out if this was true.

Like a king or a prince he wore no watch. Eddie Feathers had, in wartime, as bombs were falling about them on a quayside in Ceylon and Ross had decided to make a run for it, presented Ross with a watch, his most precious possession. It had been Eddie's father's. The watch, of course, had long disappeared, bartered probably for food, but it was not forgotten and never replaced.

On Ross's head today and every day was a size 10 brown trilby hat, also from St James's Street. Around the feet of the two men stood two leather briefcases stamped in gold with Eddie Feathers's initials. It was the class of luggage that would grow old along with the owner as he became Queen's Counsel, Judge, High Court Judge, perhaps Lord of Appeal in Ordinary, even Queen's Remembrancer, and possibly God.

Feathers would deserve his success. He was a thoroughly good, nice man, diligent and clever. He had grown up lonely, loved only by servants in Malaya. He had become an orphan of the Raj, fostered (disastrously) in Wales. He had been moved to a boarding school, had lost friends in the Battle of Britain, one of whom meant more to him than any family and whom he never spoke about. Sent back to the East as an evacuee, he had met Ross on board a leaky boat and lost him again. Eddie returned to England penniless and sick and, after a dismal time learning Law at Oxford, had been sitting underemployed in a back corridor of ice-cold

Dickensian Chambers in Lincoln's Inn (the Temple having been bombed to rubble) when he was suddenly swept to glory by the reappearance of Ross, now a solicitor carrying with him oriental briefs galore, a sack of faery gold.

Directed by Ross, Eddie began to specialise in Bomb Damage Claims, then in General Building Disputes. Almost at once Ross had him in good suits flying about the world on the way to becoming Czar (as the saying is now) of the Construction Industry. In the Far East, there began the sky-scraper boom.

And now, during the lean Attlee years post-war, Eddie was being discussed over Dinners in the Inns of Court by his peers munching their whale-meat steaks. Most of them had little else to occupy them. Litigation in the early 1950s was as rare as wartime suicide.

But there was no great jealousy. The Construction Industry is not glamorous like Slander and Libel or Crime. It is supposed to be easy, unlike Shipping or Chancery. Indeed, it comes dangerously close to Engineering, ever despised in England. It is often referred to as Sewers and Drains. Hence Filth? No – not hence Filth. Filth was an entirely affection-ate pseudonym. Eddie, or Filth, who always looked as if he'd stepped out of a five-star-hotel shower, was immaculate in body and soul. Well, almost. People got on with him, always at a distance, of course, in the English way. Having no jealousy, he inspired none. Women . . .

Ah, women. Well, women were intrigued by him. There was nothing effete about him. He was not unattractive sexu-ally. His eye could gleam. But no one made any headway.

He had no present entanglements, and there was no one to hear him talk in his sleep in the passionate Malay of his childhood.

His memory was as mysterious and private as anybody's. He knew only that his competence and his happiness were at their greatest in Far Eastern sunlight and the crash and rattle of monsoon rain, the suck and grind and roar of hot seas on white shores. It was in the East that he won most of his cases.

His only threat was another English lawyer, slightly younger and utterly different: a man who spoke no language other than English, had a degree in Engineering and some sort of diploma in Law from a Middlesbrough technical college often called 'a night school', and was bold, ugly and unstoppable, irrepressibly merry in a way a great many women and many men found irresistible. His name was Terry Veneering.

Terry Veneering was to be on the other side in the Case Edward Feathers was about to fight in Hong Kong. He was, however, on a different plane, or perhaps staying in Hong Kong already for he had a Chinese wife. Eddie was becoming expert in forgetting about his detested rival, and was concentrating now in the airport lounge on his solicitor, Ross, who was splattering a pack of playing cards from hand to hand, cutting, dealing, now and then flinging them into the air in an arc and catching them sweetly on their way down. Ross was raising a breeze.

'I wish you wouldn't do that,' said Filth. 'People are becoming irritated.'

'It's because hardly any of them are able to,' said Ross. 'It is a gift.'

'You were messing with cards the first time I met you. Why can't you take up knitting?'

'No call for woollens in Hong Kong. Find the Lady.'

'I don't want to find the bloody Lady. Where's this bloody plane? Has something gone wrong with it? They tell you nothing.'

'It shouldn't. It's the latest thing. Big square windows.'

'Excellent. Except it doesn't seem to work. The old ones were better last year. Trundling along. Screws loose. Men with oilcans taking up the carpets. And we always got there.'

'We're being called,' said Ross. He snapped the cards into a wad, the wad into a pouch, and with some gypsy sleight of hand picked up both briefcases and thumped off towards the lifts. From above, he looked like a walking hat.

Filth strode behind carrying his walking stick and the *Daily Telegraph*. At the steps up to the plane Ross, as was proper, stood back for his Counsel to pass him and Filth was bowed aboard and automatically directed to turn left to the first class. Ross, hobbling behind in the Dr Scholl's, was asked to set down the hand luggage and show his seat number.

But it was Ross who saw the cases safely stowed, changed their seats for ones that could accommodate Filth's long legs, the plane being as usual half empty, and Ross who commanded Filth's jacket to be put on a hanger in a cupboard, declined to take off his hat and who demanded an immediate refill of the complimentary champagne.

They both sat back and watched England gallop backwards,

then the delicious lurch upwards through the grey sky to the sunlit blue above.

'This champagne is second-rate,' said Ross. 'I've had better in Puerto Rico.'

'There'll be a good dinner,' said Filth. 'And excellent wine. What about your hat?'

Ross removed it with both hands and laid it on his table.

A steward hovered. 'Shall I take that from you, sir?'

'No. I keep it with me.' After a time he put it at his feet.

The dinner trolley, with its glistening saddle of lamb, was being wheeled to the centre of the cabin. Silver cutlery – real silver, Ross noted, turning the forks to confirm the hallmark – was laid on starched tray cloths. A carving knife flashed amidships. Côtes-du-Rhône appeared.

'Remember the *Breath o'Dunoon*, Albatross?' said Filth. 'Remember the duff you made full of black beetles for currants?'

Ross brooded. 'I remember the first mate. He said he'd kill me at Crib. He *wanted* to kill me. I beat him.'

'It's a wonder we weren't torpedoed.'

'I thought we *were* torpedoed. But then, I have been so often torpedoed –'

'Thank you, thank you,' roared out Filth in the direction of the roast lamb. He was apt to roar when emotionally disturbed: it was the last vestige of the terrible stammer of his Welsh childhood. 'Don't start about torpedoes.'

'For example,' said Ross, 'in the Timor Sea. I was wrecked off . . .'

But vegetables had arrived and redcurrant jelly and they munched, meditating on this and that, Ross's heavy chin a few inches above his plate. 'You ate thirty-six bananas,' he said. 'On Freetown beach. You were disgusting.'

'They were small bananas. This lamb is splendid.'

'And there'll be better to come when we've changed planes at Delhi. Back to chopsticks and the true cuisine.'

After the tray cloths were drawn and they had finished with their coffee cups, they drowsed.

Filth said that he'd have to get down to his papers. 'No – I'll fish them out for myself. You look after your hat. What do you keep in it? Opium?'

Ross ignored him.

Hot towels were brought, the pink tape round the sets of papers undone, the transcripts spread and Ross slept.

How he snores, thought Filth. I remember that on the old *Dunoon*. And he got to work with his fountain pen and a block of folio, and was soon deaf, blind and oblivious to all else. The sky that enwrapped them now blackened the windows. Below, invisible mountain ranges were speckled with pinpricks of lights like the stars all around and above them. Before long, seats were being converted into beds – not Filth's; he worked on – and blankets and warm socks were distributed. Night already.

'Brandy, sir? Nightcap?'

'Why not,' said Filth, pulling the papers together, taking off his cashmere pullover and putting on a Marks & Spencer's. A steward came to ease off his shoes.

I have seldom felt so happy, he thought, sipping the brandy, closing his eyes, awaiting sleep. I wonder if I should tell the Albatross why? No. Better wait till after Delhi.

But then: Why not? I owe him so much. Best person, just about, I've ever met. Most loyal. My salvation. I've had other salvations, but this one looks like lasting.

He watched the strange sleeping face of the dwarf, and Ross opened his eyes.

'Coleridge?'

Albert Ross looked startled.

'Coleridge, I have something to tell you.'

At once the playing cards were flying. Ross began to shuffle and deal them.

'Will you put those bloody things away?'

'Do I understand', said Ross setting them carefully down, 'that there is to be some sort of revelation?'

'Yes.'

'Much better find the Lady,' said Ross, beginning to deal again.

'I *have* found the lady, Coleridge. I have found her.'

There was silence; only the purr of the plane.

The silence lasted until Delhi and all through the stopover, the pacing in the marble first-class lounge, the buying of trinkets in the shops – Ross bought a case of blue butterflies – the resettling into Air India. Along swam the smiling, painted girls in their cheongsams. The final take-off for Hong Kong.

'So,' said Ross. 'You are about to be married. It is a revelation all right, but immaterial to your profession. Wait until you've done it as often as I have.'

Filth looked uneasy. 'You never told me any of that, Albert.'

'I consider that they are my private affairs. Who is she?'

'She'll be in Hong Kong when we get there. Waiting. Today.'

'She's Chinese?'

'No. No, a Scottish woman. But born in Tiensin. I met her – well, I've been meeting her off and on for a year or so. Whenever we come out East. The first case you got for me. In Singapore.'

'So that I'm to blame?'

'Yes. Of course. I'm very glad to say. You will, I hope, be best man at my wedding. Without that hat.'

'Her name?'

'She's called Elisabeth Macintosh. Betty. She's a good sort. Very attractive.'

'A *good sort*!' The cards again were flying. 'A *good sort*?' He was wagging his weird Johnsonian head from side to side.

'She hasn't actually accepted me yet,' said Filth. 'I've only just asked her. In a letter from Chambers sent to her hotel and marked "To await arrival". She's just passing through with a friend. They've been in Australia – or somewhere. She has had some sort of work – I'm not sure. Rather hush-hush. She's a natural traveller but not at all well off. She's at the Old Colony Hotel.'

'Never heard of it.' Without apparent volition the cards rose like liquid into a circle, and subsided.

'Look, Albert, on the whole perhaps not mention it yet. I

think she *may* accept me. Seems quite fond of me. She hasn't actually said –'

'I'm glad that she seems fond of you. It is the usual thing.'

'And I'm really very fond of her. What's the matter?'

'You haven't slept with her then?'

A steward looked away but went on listening.

'No,' cried Filth, loud and unaware. 'No, of course not. She's a lady. And I want to marry her.'

'How young?'

'I've never asked. She's a young girl. Well, she can't technically be a girl. She grew up in the war. Japanese internment camp in Shanghai. Lost both parents. Doesn't speak about it.'

'Have you ever asked her about it?'

'One doesn't intrude.'

'Edward, what does she know about *you*? That you ought to tell her? What have you talked about? Will she stay with you?'

'She's good at birds and plants. So am I. My prep school. She's very lively. Infectiously happy. Very bright eyes. Strong. Rather – muscular. I feel safe with her.' Filth looked at the throbbing structure of the plane. 'As a matter of fact,' he said, 'I would die for her.'

'Yes, I will,' the girl was saying in the shabby hotel in the backstreet, and street music playing against the racket of the mah-jong players on every open stone balcony. The overhead fan was limp and fly-spotted. On the beds were 1920s scarlet satin counterpanes with ugly yellow flowers done in stem stitch. They must have survived the war. Old wooden shutters clattered. There was the smell of the rotting lilies heaped in a yard below. Betty was alone, her friend Lizzie out somewhere, thank goodness. Betty would have hated not to be alone when she read Edward's letter. What lovely handwriting. Rather a shame he'd used his Chambers writing paper. She wondered how many rough drafts he'd made first. Transcripts. He was wedded to transcripts. This was meant to be kept.

And she would. She'd keep it for ever. Their grandchildren would leave it to a museum as a memento of the jolly old dead.

Eddie Feathers? Crikey! He does sound a bit quaint. (*Would you consider our being married, Elisabeth?*) Not exactly Romeo. More like Mr Knightley, though Mr Knightley had a question mark about him. Fortyish and always off to London alone. Don't tell me that Emma was his first. I'm wandering. I do rather wish Eddie wasn't so perfect. But of course I'll marry him. I can't think of a reason not to.

She kissed the letter and put it down her shirt.

Over the South China Sea Albert Ross was saying, 'Do you know anything about this girl? Do you think she knows a bloody thing about you?'

'I'd say I was pretty straightforward.'

'Would you! *Would* you?'

The plane lurched sideways and down. Then again sideways and down. It tilted its wings like a bird that had suddenly lost concentration and fallen asleep in the dark.

18

Though, thought Filth, the prep-school-trained ornithologist, they never do.

'Elisabeth', he said, 'makes me think of a kingfisher. She glitters and shines. Or a glass of water.'

'Oh?'

'A glass of clear water in a Scottish burn rushing through heather.'

'Good God.'

'Yes.'

'Has she ever *seen* heather? Born in Tiensin? Is she beautiful?'

Filth looked shocked. 'No, no! My goodness, no. Not at all. Not *glamorous*.'

'I see.'

'Her – presence – is beautiful.' (It must be the glass of champagne that had been served with breakfast.) 'Her soul is right.'

Ross picked up the cards. 'You are not a great connoisseur of women, Edward.'

'How do you know, Coleridge? We didn't talk about women on the *Breath o'Dunoon*.'

'So what about the Belfast tart?'

'I never told you that!'

'The shilling on the mantelpiece. You talked of nothing else when you were delirious with poisoned bananas.'

Filth in his magnificence pondered.

'You'd better tell Miss Macintosh the outcome.'

'How did you hear the outcome?'

'Oh, I know people.'

'Look here, I'm cured. I have a certificate. "VD", they called it. Peccadilloes up there on the frontier. Old as soldiers. Old as man. Mostly curable.'

'You weren't on the frontier. You went to bed with an Irish slag in a boarding house in Belfast.'

'I was sixteen.'

'Yes. Well. You were curiously unperturbed. I'm worried about your . . .'

'What?'

'Fertility.'

'For the love of God, Ross! I'm not sure I can go on knowing you.'

'*Think*, Eddie. Nobody knows you like I do.'

Below them the sun was rising from the rim of the globe. Mile-high columns of mist stood about in the air. Curtains of a giant stage. Stewardesses were clicking up the blinds, letting in one bar of sunlight after another. The canned music began. Chinese music now. Ting-tang. Sleeping bodies began to stir and stretch and yawn, and Edward Feathers smiled. Looking out, so near to landing and yet so high, he waited for the first sight of the three hundred and twenty-five islands that are called Hong Kong.

On one of them Betty Macintosh would be reading his letter. He saw her smiling and skipping about. Sweet child. So young and dear and good.

What would she have made of him on the *Breath o'Dunoon*? Young, ravaged, demented, shipwrecked? She'd have been a child then. He'd been a gaunt, sick boy, just left school. With an Adam's apple. Though women had never been scarce, from the start.

Isobel.

Nowadays women looked at him as if he were a cliff face. I'm not attractive, he thought, but they've been told there's a seam of gold about. Called money, I suppose.

'We're here,' said Ross, and Kai Tak airport was waiting below.

They swung round the harbour: the familiar landing pad that stuck out over the water like a diving board. During the war a plane a week had been lost there. Since then only one had tipped over into the harbour. But passengers, on beginning to land, always fell quiet for a moment.

'And so, Edward,' said the bright-eyed girl that night, as the red sun dropped back into the sea, 'Eddie, I will,' and she took his hand. 'I will. Yes. Thank you. I will and I will and I will.'

Somewhere in the archipelago her friend Lizzie would be drinking in a bar.

All morning she had been saying, 'Betty – you can't. It'd be a dreadful mistake.'

Finally, she had said, 'All right. I'll tell you something. I *know* him.'

'You never said! *How*? You know *Edward*?'

'See this pinhead? It's the world. The middle classes. The Empire club. It'll all be gone in a few years, and I suppose we should be glad.'

21

'You *know* Eddie?'

'Yes. In the biblical sense, too. I was wild for him. Wild. He had this quality. I don't know what it was. Probably still is. But you can't forget Teddy Feathers. He doesn't understand anyone, Bets, certainly not women. Something awful in his childhood. He's inarticulate when he's not in Court, and then you hear another voice. As you do when he's asleep – I know. He speaks Malay. D'you know he once had a horrible stammer? He's a blank to everyone except that dwarf lawyer person, and *there's* a mystery. Bets, you will be perfect for him as he becomes more and more boring. Pompous. Set in stone. Titled, no doubt. Rich as Croesus. But there's something missing. Mind, he's not sexless. He's very enjoyable. It was before I was the other way –'

'Did you ever tell him about that?'

'Good God, no! He'd be disgusted. He leaves you feeling guilty as it is, he's so pure. But there's something missing. Maybe it's his nanny – oh, Betty, *don't.*'

She said, 'Lizzie-Izz, you're jealous!'

'Probably. A bit.'

All day Betty had walked about, crossing and recrossing the city, changing twice from Hong Kong to Kowloon-side. It was Sunday, and she went into St John's Cathedral and took Communion. She got a shock when the Chinese priest changed from Cantonese to English when he administered the Bread to her. She always forgot that she was not Chinese. She walked afterwards towards Kai Tak. Planes were landing and taking off from the airport all the time.

22

She had no idea when Eddie's would arrive. The planes shrieked over the paper houses of the poor. The people there were said to be deaf.

Not noticing the noise, she wandered on among the filthy streets and came to a blistered building four storeys high with rubbish on every cement stair. She climbed up and up, noise bursting from each doorway and gallery, like feeding time at the zoo. The dear, remembered childhood chorus, the knockout smells of food and scraps. She clambered over boxes and bundles of rags and birdcages and parcels guarded by immobile individuals glaring at nothing. Rice bubbled thick on little stoves. On the third floor some Buddhist monks were chanting, and there was the smell of lamp oil, spices and smoke. On the top floor there was an antique English pram, inscribed Silver Cross, nearly blocking the apartment door which her friend Amy opened when Betty knocked, a blond and rosy child on her hip and another child imminent. She had a Bible in one hand and was holding the place in it with her thumb. Schoolfriends, they hadn't met since Amy became a missionary several years ago. She had been a dancer then.

Amy said, 'Oh. Hullo, Betty Macintosh. Come on in. There's a prayer group, but there'll be some food. Can you stay the night?' Behind her the corridor was packed with noisy people.

Inside the apartment there appeared to be no furniture except a piano where a very old Englishwoman was going hell for leather at Moody and Sankey hymns, as children of several nationalities were being fed, cross-legged on the

23

floor. The old lady began to sing to her own accompaniment. 'She's a missionary, too,' said Amy. 'But she's got Depression. We have her round here every day in case she jumps into the harbour. She lives towards the New Territories behind barbed wire and guard dogs – she has some antiques – and does it stink!'

A chair was found. Betty sat on it and was given the baby to hold while Amy went off to dollop out rice from a black pot. The old lady stopped playing and singing and began to cry, and a different surge of wailing Buddhist chant rose from the floor below. From a sort of cupboard burst a young Englishman who ran out of the apartment, leaned over the Harrods pram on the landing, and began to shout down to the monks that they could damn well give over. He was trying to work. If they wanted food, here it was, but they could stop chanting and let God have an alternative for half an hour. His Cantonese was very good. In a moment several monks in orange robes had negotiated the pram. They came into the apartment where they stood about, smiling in a row, awaiting rice.

Amy, ladle in hand, took the baby from Betty's knee and dumped it on the knee of the Depressive. It immediately began to cry, which made the Depressive stop, and Amy, holding two dishes of rice, squeezed herself down on the floor near Betty, and said, 'So?'

'Hello, Amy.'

'So, when did you get home?'

'Home? I've not had a home for years.'

'Oh, get on,' said Amy.

'I'm on holiday. Passing through. I'm drifting.'

'Alone?'

'With a girlfriend. Lizzie Ingoldby. D'you remember? Older than us, at school. Where's Nick?'

'That was Nick, yelling at the Buddhists. He's trying to write a sermon on Submission to God. He's upset. They all fall in love with him out here and he hates to disappoint a woman. By the way, we're having another.'

'I can see.'

'It will make four. And we're broke. Have you any spare money?'

'Not a bean. I'm coming into money when I'm thirty. My parents thought I might be flighty. Instead, I'm hungry.'

'Well, don't become a missionary. We're not hungry but we'd like a sideline. We're not allowed a sideline. A rich one who puts his arms round me would be nice.'

The old lady, a Mrs Baxter, had now silenced the baby with *Hymns Ancient & Modern*, and called out, 'Oh, I do agree! I am not a nun.' And began to dab her eyes. Amy passed her a very small cup of rice wine.

'We're just about all she's got,' said Amy. 'She hasn't the fare to England and there's nobody she knows there now if she even got there. So what sort of sideline have you got, clever old Elisabeth of the Enigma Variations and always top of the form, star of St Paul's and St Anne's?'

'I think – well, I think – I'm going in for a husband.'

'Oh? Really? Oh, very, *very* good. Who is it?'

'You don't know him. Well, I don't think you do. I don't know him very well, either. I came to ask you if I should do it. He's flying in tonight. I'll have to make up my mind. I'm sick of fretting on about it. By tomorrow. Maybe tonight.'

'What is he? English or Chinese? Is he Christian or ghastly agnostic? Your eyes have tears in them.'

'He's English. Christian. Not Christian like you are, full time. More like I am. Doesn't talk about it. Oh, yes, and he's already pretty rich. He'll get *very* rich. He's got the touch. He's an advocate. He'll be a judge.'

'Oh, he's in his nineties. Does he dribble?'

'No. He's quite young. He's brilliant. And he's so good-looking he finds he's embarrassed walking down the street. Thinks they belong – his looks – to a different man. He's very, very nice, Amy. And he needs me.'

'So?'

'I don't know.'

'Have you slept with him?'

'He's not the sort. I don't even know . . .'

'He's a virgin?'

'Oh, no. Not that. I've heard. In the war he was close to Queen Mary.'

'He had an affair with Queen Mary?'

They stared at each other and began to howl and laugh and roll about, as at school.

'He must be very grand,' said Amy.

'No. Oh, no. He never knows who anyone is. Social stuff doesn't interest him.'

'And you? You, you, you? D'you love him?'

'I don't know. I think so. I suppose I should but you see I'm retarded. I want the moon, like a teenager.'

26

'You *should* want the moon. Don't do it, Bets. Don't go for a forty-watt light bulb because it looks pretty. You'll get stuck with it when it goes out. You are so loyal, and you'll have to soldier on in the dark for ever afterwards.'

Mrs Baxter announced that Jesus was the Light of the World.

'That's right,' said Amy. 'Have some more wine.'

'And Him only shalt thou serve,' said Mrs Baxter.

'Amy, I must go. He may already be here. At any minute.'

'But come back. You will come back, won't you? Bring him.'

Betty tried to see Edward standing in the pools of rice in his polished shoes, the Buddhists chanting, Mrs Baxter weeping.

'I'd love your life, Amy.'

'So you say,' said Amy.

Chapter Three

And so, a few hours later, into the sea dropped the great red yo-yo sun and darkness painted out the waters of a bay. Then lights began to show, first the pricking lights under the ramparts they stood on, then more nebulous lights from boats knocking together where the fishermen lived in houses on stilts, then the lights of moving boats fanning white on black across the bay, and then across far-away bays and coastlines of the archipelago; lights of ferries, coloured lights of invisible villages and way over to the south, dim lights staining the darkness of Hong Kong itself.

Edward Feathers and Elisabeth Macintosh stood side by side, looking out, and a drum began to beat. Voices rose in a screech, like a sunset chorus of raucous birds: Cantonese and half a dozen dialects; the crashing of pots and pans, clattering pandemonium. Blue smoke rose up from the boats to the terrace of the hotel and there was a blasting smell of hot fish. Behind the couple standing looking out, waiters were beginning to spread tablecloths and napkins, setting down saucers decorated with floating lights and flowers. The last suggestion of a sun departed and the sky was speckled with a hundred million stars.

'Edward? Eddie – yes. Thank you. Yes. I will and I will and I will, but could you say something?'

Some of the older waiters would respond to Elisabeth's voice in the slow English of before the war. It was beginning to sound Old World. Proud, unflinching, Colonial. Yet the girl did not conform to it. She was bare-legged, in open-toed sandals with clean but unpainted toenails. She was wearing a cotton dress she had had for years, and hadn't thought about changing to meet her future husband. The time in the Shanghai detention centre had arrested her body rather than matured her, and she would still have been recognised by her school first-eleven hockey team.

Edward looked down at the top of her curly head, rather the colour of his own. 'Chestnut', they call it. Conker-colour. Red. Our children are bound to have red hair. Red hair frightens the Chinese. Our children'll have to go Home to England, if we settle here. If we have any children . . .

She said, '*Edward*? Please?'

At last, then, he embraced her.

'We must get back,' he said, and on the ferry again across the harbour they sat close together, but not touching, on a slatted seat. Nearby sat a pasty young Englishman who was being stroked and sighed over by a Chinese girl with a yearning face. She was plump and pale, gazing up at him, whispering to him, kissing him all the time below the ear. He flicked at the ear now and then as if there were a fly about, but he was smiling. The ferry chugged and splashed. The Englishman looked proud and content. 'She's a great cook, too,' he called in their direction. 'She can do a great mashed potato. It's not all that rice.'

At Kowloon-side Edward and Elisabeth walked a foot or so apart to his hotel, climbed the marble steps and passed through the flashing glass doors. Inside among the marble columns and the lilies and the fountains, Edward lifted a finger towards the reception desk and his room key was brought to him.

'There's a party now.'

'When? Whose?'

'Now. Here. It's tomorrow's Judge. It's going to be a long Case, and he's a benevolent old stick. He likes to kick off with a party. Both sides invited. Leaders, juniors, wives, girl-friends, fiancées. And courtesans for flavour.'

'Must we go?'

'Yes. I don't much want to, but you don't refuse.'

When he looked down at her she saw how happy he was.

'Have I time to change?'

'No. It will have begun. We'll just show our faces. Your clothes are fine. I have something for you to wear, as it happens. I'll go up and change my jacket and I'll bring it down.'

'Shall I come up to the room with you?'

The new, easy, happy Edward faltered. 'No. I don't think they care for that here. I'll be back in ten minutes. I'll order you some tea.'

'It's a strange betrothal,' Betty told the lily-leaf-shaped tray, the shallow cup, the tiny piece of Battenburg cake and the cress sandwich so small that a breeze from the fountains might blow it away. A trio behind her was playing Mozart. Two Chinese, one Japanese, very expert and scornful. She remembered how people in England used to say that no Oriental would ever be able to play Mozart. Just like they used to say that there would never be Japanese pilots because the Japanese are all half blind behind dark glasses. She was all at once overcome by the idiotic nature of mankind and began to laugh. God must feel like me, she thought. Oh, I love Hong Kong. Could we live here? Could Edward?

Here he came now, washed and shaved in a clean shirt and linen jacket, loping over from the lift, smiling like a boy (I'm going to be with this person all my life!) and he dropped a little cloth bag into her lap and she took out from it the most magnificent string of pearls.

'Yours,' he said. 'They're old. Someone gave them to me. When I was sixteen. In the war. Just in time. She died a few minutes later. She was lying next to me under a lifeboat on deck. We were limping Home up the Irish Sea – everybody sick and dying. She was very old. Raj spinster. Whiskery. Brave. Type that's gone. She said, "One day you can give them to your sweetheart."'

31

She thought: He's not cold at all. Then, Oh, OH!! The pearls are wonderful. But they're not what matters.

'There's a condition, Elisabeth.'

'About the pearls?'

'Certainly not. They are yours for ever. You are my sweetheart. But this marriage, our marriage . . .'

'Hush,' she said. 'People are listening. Later.'

'No – NOW,' he roared out in the way he did; and several heads turned. 'This marriage is a big thing. I don't believe in divorce.'

'You're talking about divorce before you've proposed.'

Mozart behind them sang out, *Aha! Bravo! Goodbye!* And the trio stood up and bowed.

'Elisabeth, you must never leave me. That's the condition. I've been left all my life. From being a baby, I've been taken away from people. Raj orphan and so on. Not that I'm unusual there. And it's supposed to have given us all backbone.'

'Well, I know all that. I am an orphan, too. My parents suffered.'

'All our parents suffered for an ideology. They believed it was good for us to be sent Home, while they went on with ruling the Empire. We were all damaged even though we became endurers.'

('May I take your tray, madam?')

'It did not destroy me but it made me bloody unsure.'

'I will never leave you, Edward.'

'I'll never mention any of this again.' His words began to stumble. 'Been sent away all my life. Albert Ross saved me. So sorry. Came through. Bad at sharing feelings.'

'Which, dear Eddie, if I may say so, must be why you haven't yet proposed to me.'

'I thought I had –'

'No. Your Chambers stationery has. Not you. I want to hear it from you. In your words. From your lips.' (She was happy, though.)

'Marry me, Elisabeth. Never leave me. I'll never ask again. But *never* leave me.'

'I'll never leave you, Edward.'

A waiter swam by and scooped up her tray though she called out, 'Oh, no!'

Bugger, she thought, I've had nothing all day but that rice at Amy's. Then: I shouldn't be thinking of cake.

In the lift on the way up to the Judge's party, her bare toes inside the sandals crunching the sand of the distant sunset harbour, she thought: Well, now I know. It won't be romantic, but who wants that? It won't be passion, but better without, probably. And there will be children. And he's remarkable and I'll grow to love him very much. There's nothing about him that's *un*lovable.

They stood together now at the far end of the corridor where the Judge had his suite. They could see the open doors, gold and white. The noise of the party inside rose in a subdued roar.

Edward said, 'Unclutch those pearls. I want to put them round your neck.' He took them, heavy and creamy, into both hands and held them to his face. 'They still smell of the sea.'

She said, 'Oh, ridiculous,' and laughed, and he at last kissed her very gravely in full view of the waiters round the distant door. She saw that his eyes brimmed with tears.

Why, the dear old thing, she thought.

Chapter Four

The Judge was standing just inside the doors of his suite to welcome his guests, and ostentatiously waving about a glass of Indian tonic water to make clear to everyone that tomorrow morning he would be in Court. He was a clever, abstracted little man with a complexion pale and freckled like cold porridge. He had been born in the East, and his skin still didn't seem to know what to make of it. His wife, Dulcie, much younger and here with him on a visit, was vague and dumpy in paisley-patterned silk. The arrival of the up-and-coming Edward and the unconventional-looking young woman appeared to mean little to either of them. The Judge was looking everywhere around.

'Aha, yes. Eddie Feathers,' said the Judge (he was known as Pastry Willy). 'Well done. Arrived safely. Good flight? Well, don't let me monopolise you. We'll be head-on for months. Sick of the sight of each other. I've said exactly the same to the other side for the same reason. They're all over there.'

Gales of laughter were arising from across the room and

there was the impression of someone bigger than the rest buffooning about. He had a flap of flaxen hair.

'I can't remember how well you know Veneering?'

'Quite well.'

Pastry Willy quickly looked away. Something about a mutual and inexplicable loathing.

'May I introduce Elisabeth Macintosh?' said Edward. 'She is about to become my wife.'

'Delighted, delightful,' said the Judge, and his wife Dulcie blinked at the gingham dress and pearls.

Elisabeth leaned forward and kissed Pastry Willy on the cheek. 'Hello, Uncle Willy. I'm Betty Macintosh.' She kissed him again on the other cheek.

'Oh, my goodness! Little Betty! Joseph's girl!'

'Father died,' she said, and disappeared into the crowd.

'But this is splendid! Splendid, Feathers! I used to read fairy tales to her on my knee.' Edward was hurrying after her. 'In Tiensin!'

'Elisabeth!' He caught up with her. 'You kissed Willy?'

'Well, I knew him when I was seven,' she said.

In the heart of the throng Edward, looking joyous, began to declare to left and right, 'Hello, my – my fiancée.'

The room became more crowded still, the talk all London Inns of Court and how the Colony was awash this month with English lawyers. A drift of excited wives just off the plane surged by in new silk dresses they'd already had time to buy, their hair and lipstick all in place and shiny. A lovely Chinese woman in pale yellow with chandelier earrings was reclining on a chaise longue. She had a face of perpetual ennui. From the corner of the room where the noise was wildest, the flaxen-headed man separated himself from his friends, roaring with laughter. He was wearing khaki shorts and a khaki shirt, which made him seem not eccentric but ahead of fashion and in the sartorial know. 'No, not that way,' Edward commanded Elisabeth, and the man with the bright hair cried out, 'Oh, God! It's Old Filth!' Then he saw Elisabeth in the pearls and gingham and stood perfectly still.

'I'm Veneering,' he said to her, 'Terry Veneering.' His eyes were bright light blue.

Elisabeth thought: And it is just one hour too late.

'Come and meet –' Edward was steering her away. 'You must meet my clerk and – I don't see Ross anywhere yet. I hope you're going to like him. I'll tell you – oh, hello! *Hello*! Tony, Desmond. Safe here, all of us. This is –'

But Elisabeth had slid away. Through some glass doors on to an airy balcony she had spotted a glitter of dishes. Her holiday money she'd used up in Australia, and for the past week she and Lizzie had been eating nothing much except noodles and deep-fried prawns off the market stalls. At the end of this frugal day of celebration (when she'd thought there'd be a feast, looking out over the sunset harbour), she was ravenous and – with a percipience she would keep and be thankful for throughout her coming life – she'd noticed that Edward hadn't mentioned dinner. And she knew that after the party he would find urgent work to do for the next day.

*

Belshazzar's feast was laid out on white cloths on the balcony, a row of robotic waiters standing behind.

'I'm your first customer,' she said, and with faint disapproval one of them handed her a plate and she passed down the buffet alone, helping herself hugely to crab and lobster mayonnaise. Oh, glory!

She sat down alone at an empty side table with a long white cloth to the floor, stretched her sandy feet beneath it and touched something that squeaked.

Putting her chopsticks neatly down, she lifted a corner of the tablecloth and saw a boy cross-legged on the marble, crunching a lobster. He had black Chinese hair that stood up spikily in an un-oriental way. His eyes were blue.

'Good evening,' said Elisabeth. 'Do you usually eat underneath tables?'

'Sometimes they let me in ahead of time. I get hungry at my father's parties, too.'

'Oh, I'm always hungry,' she said. 'But I'll stay in the open tonight. Who are you? I'm Betty Macintosh.'

'Like a raincoat?' He licked each finger thoroughly before holding out his hand. 'I'm Harry Veneering. I'm an only child. My father is a very famous barrister. He works out here a lot of the time but I'm at school in England. I'm flying back to school tonight.'

'Is the lobster then altogether wise? Do you think?'

'Oh, yes, thanks. I'm never sick. I can eat anything. I'm like my father. My mother eats just about nothing, ever.'

'Where are you at school in England?'

'Near London. It's a prep school. For Eton, of course. My father being who he is.'

'Is he the one in the shorts?'

'Yes. He says if you are anybody you can wear what you like anywhere. Some lord or duke told him. Or maybe it was a prime minister. He's a terrible, terrible inside-out snob, my dad, and he's very, very funny.'

'Ought you to discuss your father with a stranger?'

'Oh, yes. He's fun. He's just a joke. And very, very brilliant.'

'I've seen him. Yellow hair?'

'Yes. It's gross. But it's not dyed. I've got my mother's hair. She's the one with the long earrings.'

'You have your father's eyes.'

'Yes.' He looked at her from across the small table where he was now attacking the crabmeat. 'He's a hypnotist. That's why he wins absolutely every one of his Cases.'

'*Oh*, no,' she said, '*Oh*, no. I am about to be married to another barrister and he wins Cases too and some of them against your father. And he *never* boasts. And he wasn't at Eton. And he's not a snob of any kind, ever. How old are you, and why are you arguing about matters beyond your understanding?'

'I'm nine. I'm small, but I expect to grow. My dad says boys grow to their feet and my feet – look at them – they're vast. I suppose you're going to marry Mr Feathers. Did you know he's called Old Filth? It's because he's so clean and so clever. Well, of course he is *fairly* clever.'

'You don't need to tell me about my future husband. It's

pert. Now then, come over here and bring that big table napkin with you. I'll clean you up. And remember, you are talking to the new Mrs Edward Feathers.'

'"Mrs Feathers" sounds like a hen.' And the child came over and shut his eyes, presenting his silky Chinese face to her as she dipped the dinner napkin in cold water and mopped up the mayonnaise from round his mouth. He opened his blue eyes and said, 'I know, I absolutely know I've seen you before. I didn't mean to be rude. I love hens.'

'No,' she said. 'I don't believe we've met before.'

'If you're ever back in England,' he said, 'would you like to come to my school sports days? I'm very good. I win everything and there's never anybody to see me because my parents are always somewhere else. Such as out here.'

'I should have to ask their permission.'

'Oh, it'll be all right. The school won't mind. I could say you're my nanny.'

She looked at him.

'What's the matter? You'd look exactly right. My mother's supposed to be the most beautiful woman in Hong Kong, you know.'

'That must be very difficult for her,' said Elisabeth.

The languid Chinese woman of the chaise longue was all at once standing behind them, holding a champagne glass round its rim in the tips of her fingers. The fingers of her other hand balanced her against the wall.

People were now crowding in for the buffet and the waiters were coming to life. Behind Elsie Veneering stood

Veneering. Veneering was looking at Elisabeth's unlined face, his wife at Elisabeth's unpainted sandy toenails.

'Harry,' said Elsie. 'It's time to go. Introduce me to your friend.'

'She's Miss Macintosh, she belongs to Mr Feathers. She's going to marry him. This is my mother.'

'*Marrying*?' Elsie's eyes were black and still. 'What secrets! We all rather suspected . . . How kind of you to talk to Harry. Have you children already? Grandchildren?'

'Oh yes,' said Elisabeth. 'I have twenty-seven grandchildren and I'm only twenty-eight years old.'

Elsie looked out of her depth but Harry laughed and fell on Elisabeth like a puppy. 'You will come, won't you? Come to my school? On sports day?'

'Only if your mother and father will let me.'

'There'll be no sports days at all if you don't tuck your shirt in your shorts and get smartened up. We've not finished your packing yet and the plane goes at midnight. Your mother needs a rest.' Veneering's voice was all right. OK. Just a trace of elocution lessons, maybe?

'Aren't you taking me? Dad? You always take me to the airport.' The boy who had looked as if he could outface a battalion crumpled into a baby and began to cry.

'Can't this time,' said Veneering. 'Work to be done for tomorrow. Sorry, guv'nor.'

'Why didn't you do the bloody work instead of coming to this awful party?' And biffing everyone out of his way, the child kicked out at his yellow-headed father and ran from the Judge's apartment.

Veneering stood looking at Elisabeth and Elsie drifted away.

'He must learn to travel alone,' said Veneering. 'Hundreds of them still do. Hardens them up. It's in the British genes.'

'What rubbish you talk,' said Elisabeth.

'They travel first class. Well looked-after. Met at the other end. We take a lot of trouble. Not like in your old man's time.'

'It's a fourteen-hour flight. And there's a change of plane in India.'

'He's a self-reliant little beast. He's done it before.'

'If you ever need anyone to meet him, we'll probably be living in London at first. I should like to. Please.'

'I hear you're marrying Old Filth. It's the sensation of the party. "Who is she, my dear?" No – he'd never let you have anything to do with a son of mine. We don't get on. He thinks I'm common. So when did he get rid of his stammer and manage to ask you?'

'About three hours ago.'

'Is he weighing up your acceptance? Considering your sentence? I can see that *you* are.'

She stood up. 'You are as vulgar as they say you are.' She handed him her empty plate, crumpling his son's dinner napkin on top of it as if he were a waiter, and walked away.

Chapter Five

She had been right about dinner. A junior in his team had asked Edward for a consultation after the party. It might make a vital difference to the Case. Edward would of course walk her back to her hotel first.

'Will we meet later?'

'I never know how long –'

'Edward, we've not been engaged for a day yet. Can't you even stop for some dinner? I didn't see you eating anything. We've said so little –'

'Not hungry. My clock's not settled yet, it's the middle of the night, I think.' He took her arm above the elbow and said, 'Anyway, I'm too excited.'

'Oh! Oh, well. Eddie, come to my room afterwards. At the Old C. It's number 182. I'll be alone. Lizzie's out.'

'Rather not promise. The end of the week will be ours for two full days. Then we have all the years we're going to live.'

He dropped her outside her hotel, which was pulsing with lights and screeching music.

'Well, goodnight, my future husband who doesn't ever kiss me.'

'Well, certainly not here. You know I love you. I always will. Thank you. Please live for ever. Stop me from being a bloody bore. I can't help working. It's been a safety valve since school. Device for not thinking. But I'll be all right now. Always. We'll have a long, long honeymoon when this Case is out of the way.'

He kissed her like a brother.

Her room was unlocked and she had to turn out four uni-formed room-boys who were lying on the floor and on the beds watching her tiny flickering black-and-white television. Lizzie must have turned the *Room Free* label the wrong way round instead of to *Do Not Disturb*. Lizzie's reading of Cantonese was getting hazy. There was a musky smell in the room and Elisabeth opened the window, turned off the tele-vision and the lights and the air-conditioning. Warm harbour smells floated in. The water pipes along the walls clanked to the rhythm of somebody's shower above. She took off the pearls and put them on a chair. She picked up the yellowing finger-marked breakfast menu and then thought, no, she'd order in the morning. She only needed sleep.

About midnight she woke in panic. The sky above was throbbing with planes. The boy Harry would be at the air-port now. No, he'd already be in the air, sitting in his first-class seat. 'Flying out at midnight.' To be hoped that the mother . . . The mother had looked drunk. You'd think the

44

father would have cancelled that Con. An only child. Will Edward cancel a Consultation for a child? She decided, no. But there will be me.

Our children will always have me.

Where's Lizzie? Secret life. Always had. All these secrets. She thought of the codes at Bletchley Park in the mild English countryside. We took it so lightly. Secrets. Elisabeth slept now against the madhouse clamour of Kowloon. Blank. Jet lag. Still partly in Sydney. Hole in the air, *c'est moi*. Ought to be better at all this. Calmer. I am getting married. I'm twenty-eight.

In a dream she was informing her long-dead and always shadowy parents not to worry. She was back on the blistered floor of the Camp. The dust. Her father's voice suddenly boomed out at her, 'There'll be money when you're thirty. Do nothing hasty.' His ribcage had stuck out. His nose sharp in the skull. 'I'm quite safe,' she shouted. 'I'm doing all right.'

In the morning she woke to Lizzie's radio playing beside the other bed and sat up bleary and tousled blinking across to where Lizzie lay prone. The radio rattled on in Cantonese.

'Lizzie-Izz! You're back! Where were you? I've something . . .'

'Shut up a minute. There's terrible news.'

'Oh. What news?'

'Plane crash. Early this morning. Over the Indian Ocean. It broke in two.'

Elisabeth was out of bed and dressing, 'Which?'

45

'Which what?'

'Plane. Airline. Going where?'

'British Airways, to Heathrow. The new design. A lot of children flying home to boarding school. What *are* you doing?'

Elisabeth was in her clothes. She did not do her hair or wash or look in the glass. She felt for her sandals by the bed, ran into the bathroom, ran out again, pulling up her knickers. She left the rope of pearls lying on the chair. She did not look for her purse. She ran from the room.

'I think actually they said it happened after it had left Rome,' Lizzie called, but Elisabeth was out of hearing.

Elisabeth ran into the street, on to the quay, ran across the roads in the drumming relentless Monday morning crowds that marched to work in their thousands, not looking at her, not speaking, not touching, not stumbling, and nor did she. She ran up the marble steps of the Peninsular Hotel and the bellhop boys in their white uniforms and pillbox hats pulled back the glass doors and blinked as she passed by.

Beside the fountain she stopped. The white piano on the dais was covered with a cloth and the gold music stands were folded up. She ran to the lifts and eyes turned from her in embarrassment, two immaculate men at the reception desk looking pointedly away. Somewhere above her in the hotel Edward would be getting up, thinking of the coming day in Court. It never occurred to her to ask for him.

She didn't know the number of the Veneerings' rooms

and asked the lift boy who said 'Suite Number One' but looked uncertain about taking her there. 'It's urgent,' she said. 'It's about a legal Case in the Courts.' He looked at her wild hair and crumpled dress.

But the lift rolled up, the gates slid open and she was running towards the double doors of Suite Number One and ringing the bell. She rang and rang.

The door at last was opened by a maid – no, by a nanny. One of the old amahs in black and white, her face gaunt. Behind stood Terry Veneering. And beside him stood Harry.

'We missed the plane,' the boy shouted. 'I'm still here. Mum passed out and we missed it. And one just like it crashed in the Med.' He flung himself on Elisabeth.

The amah vanished and Veneering said, 'Harry – quick. Go and tell them, Miss Macintosh needs some coffee. Go on. Go *on*.'

Then he stepped forward and took her hands and led her inside.

'No, no, I won't come in,' she said. 'It's all right now. I don't need to come in.'

His clownish face of the night before looked thin and white, his blue eyes exhausted. His hands holding hers shook. 'I thought so, too,' he said. 'But it wasn't his.'

'Must go back,' she said. 'Find Edward. Tell friend. Isobel. All right now. I'm all right now.'

'Stop crying.'

'I must be mad,' she said.

'I'll send a car for you tonight. Your hotel the Old C? I'll send a car at six-thirty. Look. Stop. He's all right. It wasn't his flight. Sing *Te Deum* and *Laudamus*. Elisabeth, *it was a different plane.*'

'Yes. Yes, I will sing – I'll sing for ever.'

'You met him – shut up or I'll shake you – you met him for about half an hour. He's mine, you know, not yours. Soon you'll have your own.'

'Yes. I can't understand. It must be hysteria. I'm never, never – Oh, but thank God. Thank God, Terry!'

'Six-thirty,' he said, shutting the door on her.

Chapter Six

She went out. She did not telephone Edward or wait for him to ring her, or explain anything to Lizzie who had again vanished. She went to a small, expensive shop and with the end of her money, labelled 'emergencies', she bought a dress.

The girl selling was shivering with cold because of the new, Western-style air-conditioning. She looked ill and resentful. Elisabeth moved the ready-made silk dresses along the rails and found her fingertips covered with oil. She showed them to the sneezing girl, who at first looked away in denial. Then, when Elisabeth said in Cantonese, 'Please take a cloth to the rails at once!' went to get one and at the same moment Elisabeth saw a sea-green silk, the dress of a lifetime. She held her black oily fingers out to let the girl clean her hands and when the girl had finished said, 'I would like that one.' The girl shrugged and moved her hands in a disenchanted gesture that Elisabeth might want to try it on and Elisabeth said, 'No, thank you. It will be perfect. Have you shoes to match?' She paid for it (a price) and walked back towards the hotel room. It was still empty of Lizzie, and there was no message light on the bedside telephone. She stood the stiff paper bag on her bed and went to find a hairdresser.

The hairdresser preened above her head.

'Is it for an occasion?'

'I don't know. Well, yes, I'm going out tonight.'

The hairdresser smiled and smiled, dead-eyed. Elisabeth had the notion that somewhere there was dislike.

'Would you like colour?'

'I don't know.'

'Would you like to be more *seriously* red?'

'No. No, not at all.' (Am I making sense?) 'Just wash my hair, please. Take the aeroplane out of it.'

'*Aeroplane* out of it.' Silly giggle.

High on the wall above the line of basins, probably unnoticed for years, was a studio photograph, from before the war, of an English woman of a certain age, her hair sculpted into marcel waves, her ageing manicured hand all rings. And she was resting her cheek against it. Her mouth was dark and sharp with lipstick, her fingernails dark with varnish. Her smile was benevolent but genuine and sweet, and she had signed her name across the corner with *I shall remember you all*. She was so like Elisabeth's mother's Bridge-playing friends in old Tiensin that for a moment Elisabeth smelled the dust of her early childhood that had settled on everything without and within, covered her mother's dressing-table mirrors, the long parchment scrolls on the walls, the tea tray with cups and silver spoons, the little grey butterfly cakes, the cigarette cases and cigar lighters and dried grasses in china vases. Memory released an instant image, and sound too, for she heard her mother's laugh as the amah carried her into the room to sit quietly at her mother's feet for half an hour, as the four ladies gazed at their cards and smoked their cigarettes. Her mother would look at her sometimes to check that she was tidy, and she would smile back, at her mother in the silk tea gown, silk stockings, the boat-shaped silk shoes, a diamond ring (where had it gone?) glinting through the dust in the shaft of sunlight through the blinds.

'Who is that woman?'

The hairdresser looked up at the photograph. 'Oh, it will be a client from before the war. Long ago.'

'Can you read her name?'

A long giggle. 'No, no! We must take it down. It is old. The frame is very old-fashioned. The salon will be modernised soon.'

'She must have liked you all. The frame is expensive. Was she the Governor's wife?'

All the girls laughed. The embarrassed, tinkling laughter.

'There are fly spots on it. We must take it down.'

'I think she gave it to you before she left for Home. Maybe when the war began. Before the Japanese.' They laughed again, watching her. She saw that one girl was Japanese. Elisabeth's hair was being dried by a new-fangled hand-held blower, like a gun. The woman would have sat for over half an hour under a metal helmet that roared in her reddening ears while she wrote letters on her knee or drifted

51

among copies of *Country Life* or *The Royal Geographical Magazine* or *John o'London's* – happy, loving her warm unhurried life, sure of the future, certain that she and her country were admired. She would always have left a tip, but unostentatiously, and at Christmas – but not at the Chinese New Year – she'd arrive with little presents for everyone wrapped in paper printed with mistletoe and holly, which none of the girls had ever seen. Little Christmas puddings and mince pies that would all be thrown away. How do I know all this?

'She is like my mother.'

'We must take it down.'

The hairdresser brought her some tea.

Back at the Old Colony there was still no message from Edward so the Case must by now be groaning into life: a Case about land reclamation. Edward was for the architects, Veneering for the contractors. The villagers living on the doomed land were for neither, and nobody represented them except the legendary monsters and serpents that lurked in the depths below the site which was at present a marsh where they had always wallowed in the imagination, seeking whom they might devour. The projected dam would produce water for the new Hong Kong which would arrive years and years later, after the handover. The villagers came out after dark to appease the monsters with offerings and saucers of milk. In the morning the Western engineers removed the untouched offerings. Nothing was getting done.

Elisabeth, in her frowsty bedroom, the beds still not

made, sent for a room-service lunch and when it came did not want it. She slept, and woke at six o'clock. No phone messages, no word from Edward or Lizzie. She combed her new shiny hair and thought of the photograph of the virtuous woman who looked like her mother. Then she took the sea-green dress and slid it on. There was a small, matching, sea-green purse on a string. She slipped it over her shoulder. Then she put on her evening shoes. Pale, silk, high-heeled sandals. Then she looked out of the window.

('I'll send a car. Six-thirty.')

It had been a time so early in the morning, half in dream, half in nightmare. Perhaps it had all been imagined.

Only hours ago she had been all set to become the next reincarnation of a virtuous woman, like the one in the benevolent photograph. She had stood beside her man – and how her parents would have approved of Edward Feathers – watching the stars in the heavens, thinking that she would tell her children about how she had said 'I will' and had meant it. She saw her mother's face, imprisoned in the emptiness of Empire and diplomacy.

A cab was standing by itself without lights across the road from the Old Colony. She turned the notice in Chinese characters on her door to *Do Not Disturb*. She left no message. She took the lift down. She carried only the little green purse. It had her passport in it and her final travellers'-cheque ticket strip, but not her return ticket to England.

As she walked over to the dark cab, the driver got out and opened the passenger door. He said, 'Veneering?' and she said, 'Yes.'

They turned quickly away from the lights and quays, then inland. As they climbed, the traffic and people thinned and they drove towards the New Territories among cities of unfinished blocks of workers' flats, all in darkness, waiting for the New Age. The road curved and climbed, flattened and then climbed again. It climbed into trees, through trees and then into thick woods.

Woods?

She had not known about the woods of Hong Kong. Woods were for lush landscapes. She had believed that outside the city all would be sandy and bare. The cab plunged now deep into a black forest. The sky was gone and the road levelled and began to drop down again. The cab turned on to an unmade-up track. Small dancing lights began to appear, around them, like a huge entourage, the moving shadows of hundreds of people carrying the lights in their hands.

The shadows did not rest. Sometimes they came up close to the cab. They were moving, sometimes quite close to the cab's closed windows. They were in twos and threes, not speaking. Not one head turned. They even seemed unaware of the cab, which was moving through them now quite fast, but still silent, the driver never once flashing his lights or sounding his horn. Nobody moved out of their way. Nobody turned his head. There seemed to be a white mist near the ground and the cab became very hot.

The strangeness of the crowded forest was its silence.

To left and right in the trees, a little off the road, a bright light would now and then shine out, then vanish, masked by trees and trees. There must be big houses up there, she thought, rich men's second homes. She had seen the sort of thing long ago in Penang, most of the year empty, shadowy palaces locked inside metal armour lattice and on the gates the warning with a zigzag sign saying *Danger of Death*, blazing out in English and Chinese and Malay.

The hosts of the shadows paid no attention to the houses hidden in the trees. The shadows swam altogether around the cab in a shoal. They concentrated on the dark. They became like smoke around her in the forest and she began to be afraid.

I want Edward. He has no idea where I am. Nor have I.

The driver's little Chinese head did not turn, and he did not speak when she leaned forward and tapped his shoulder and shouted at him in Cantonese, 'Will it be much longer? Please tell me where I am. In God's name.'

Instead, he swung suddenly off the road, obliterating the moving shadows, and up a steeper track. After a time, a glow appeared from, apparently, the top of some tree. In front of the light the cab swung round full circle and stopped.

The light was glowing in a small wooden house that seemed to be on stilts with tree branches growing close all round it. There was some sort of ladder and a gate at the bottom bore the electric charge logo and *Danger of Death*. *All admittance forbidden.*

She looked up at the top of the ladder and saw that a wooden cabin seemed held in a goblet of branches. Its doors stood open and light now flowed down the ladder.

Veneering was beside the cab. He opened the door and took her hand. He stood aside for her at the ladder's foot and at the top, she looked down at him and saw that behind him in the clearing the cab was gone.

So was the silent, shadowy multitude and so were all the dotted lights of houses among the trees. This house seemed less a house than an organic growth in the forest, sweet-smelling, held in the arms of branches. Veneering shut the door behind them and began to take off her green dress.

Chapter Seven

The next morning *Do Not Disturb* was still hanging from the door handle of room 182, the beds still unmade, unslept in. There was the untouched chaos of scattered clothes and belongings, the smell of yesterday's scent. Nobody there. And no light flashing from the bedside telephone. No messages pushed under the door.

Perhaps no time had passed since yesterday morning. The hairdresser, the green dress, the taxi standing waiting, the strange journey, the glorious night, the dawn return with the black cab again standing waiting in the trees, perhaps all fantasy? A dream of years can take a second.

But I'm not a virgin any more. I know that all right. *And* it's about time. Oh, Edward! Saint Edward, where were you? Why wasn't it you? Pulling off the dress, she stuffed it in the waste-paper basket. She made the dribbling shower work and stood under it until it had soaked away the hours of the sweltering, wonderful night, until her hair lay flat and brown and coarse. It's like a donkey's hair. I am not beautiful. Yet he thought so. Who was it? Oh! It *must* have been Edward! I'm marrying him. He hates – she couldn't say the name. I've been bewitched. Then, thinking of the night, she moaned with pleasure. No, it was you. Not Eddie. Eddie was preparing the Case. He had no time. Yet you had time. The same Case.

And it's always going to be like this. She watched, through the window behind the shower, white smoke puffing up from the air-conditioning into the blue sky. His work will always come first. He'll sign and underline and ring for it to be collected by the typists, before he comes home to me. And where is he? And Lizzie? I'm alone here now. I can't stand here all day, naked. My new, used, happy body. I suppose I should sleep now. I must need sleep, but I've never felt so awake. I'll ring Amy.

'Yes?'

In the background to Amy's voice was a hornet's nest of howling and shouting.

'I must see you, Amy. I have to see you. *Please*!'

'I'll come now. I'll do the school run and then I'll drive in. What's wrong?'

'I'll tell you. Well, not *wrong*. Well, yes – wrong.'

Amy's tin-can car appeared in less than half an hour outside the Old Colony, stopping where last night's cab had stopped. And this morning's. Elisabeth saw it, put on some cotton trousers and a shirt, and ran out. The alternative had been the crumpled cotton check or the green silk in the trash basket. She fell into the clattering car and, as they drove away, said, 'Oh, Amy! Thank God!' Amy had less than an inch of space between herself and the steering wheel. The coming child inside her was kicking. You could see it kicking if you knew about such things. Betty, who didn't know, sat staring ahead.

'Where are we going, Amy? This isn't your way home.'

'No, it's my day for health-visiting. New babies. Home births. I'll say you're my assistant. You can carry a clipboard. Now then, what's the matter?'

'I can't actually tell you. Not yet. I've just got in. I was out all night.'

'Sleeping with Eddie Feathers? Well, about time. That I will say.'

'No. No. He won't do it. He thinks if it's serious, you don't do it before marrying.'

'He said this?'

'Not actually. But he sort of indicates.'

'Well,' she said. 'It's a point of view. Mine, as a matter of fact. And Nick's. But we couldn't stick to it. So who were you with on the night you became engaged? You'd better tell me. Oh, we're here. Get out and I'll tell you how to behave. Then tell me what's going on.'

They were on a cemented forecourt of what looked like an overhead parking block ten storeys high. 'Take the clipboard. Walk behind me with authority. OK? We are weighing and measuring babies born at home. Every family will greet us with a glass of tea. If there is no tea it will be a glass of water. If there is no water then it will be an empty glass. Whichever is handed to you, you greet it as if it were champagne. OK?'

Inside the rough building among the shadowy wooden joists Elisabeth was reminded of the unseen people of the wood. At doorways they were bowed to, and tightly wrapped babies were presented, unwrapped and hung up by Amy from a hook above a little leather hammock. Like meat, thought Elisabeth. The baby was examined, peered at with a torch, tapped and patted, then measured and returned. The mother or grandmother – it could have been either – bowed and offered the glass. The babies' eyes shone black and narrow, and looked across at Elisabeth with the knowledge of Methuselah. She caught one proud young mother's glance and smiled in congratulation. 'Beautiful,' she said, and the mother made a proud disclaimer.

'That last one will die,' said Amy as they walked back to the car. 'We'll go home and I'll get you some breakfast. Let me hear your earth-shattering experiences with your substitute future husband.'

'He wasn't. I told you.'

'Then who was it?'

'Someone else. I'd just met him.'

'Ye gods! Here, help me.' She was unloading the back of the car of the paraphernalia of the maternity run. 'Met him *here*? In Hong Kong?'

'Yes. I think it was hypnosis.'

Weights, measures, bottles were heaped in Elisabeth's arms.

'Rubbish, it was lust. It was natural desire. Or maybe it was only resentment,' said Amy.

'How do you know?'

'I know because you told me, yesterday, that your marriage

60

frightened you, because it meant you would never know passion. You did it to have something to remember and to have known desire.'

'No, it was love. I'm not excusing myself. Edward will never know. It is love.'

'Elisabeth, what *are* you doing?'

'Is it so wrong to want a glorious memory?'

'It's sentimental and obscene. You won't like yourself for it in the end. You don't like yourself now.'

'I never thought you were a puritan, Amy.'

'Well, you've learned something. I am.'

'After the way you went on at school.'

'That was ten years ago.'

'So you have been purified by Nick?'

Amy was rolling from side to side up the dirty stairwell, trying to support the unborn baby as it kicked to get clear of her ribcage and slide into the world. From above came the wailing of apparently inconsolable children and the voice of a roaring man.

A saffron monk stuck his head out of his doorway as they passed, his hairless shining face determinedly blissful. He asked if he could eat with them. 'No,' said Amy. 'There's too much going on,' and the monk blissfully retired.

'Where in *hell* –' shouted Nick at their open door. 'You've been hours. We're going mad.'

Mrs Baxter, in a rocking chair, held an unhappy bundle. 'I'm afraid she's wet again.' An untouched bottle of formula stood near, untouched, that is, except by flies. 'It's time to get Emily back from school.'

'Well, here's the car keys,' said Amy, picking the baby out of Mrs Baxter's bony lap, dropping the nursing gear, scooping another child out of Nick's struggling arms. 'Oh, and can you give Bets a lift back to the Old Col?'

'Bets?' Nick took a hold, looked at her and switched on the polite. 'So sorry. Don't think we've met. Are you new here?'

'I'm passing through.'

'We were at school,' said Amy.

'Oh. *Excellent.* Sorry about the scenes of married bliss. Didn't see you there, ha-ha. You'll want to be off.'

'No. I don't want to go.' She looked at Nick in his plastic dog collar. 'Amy, I don't know what to do.'

'Pray you're not pregnant,' said Amy, also behaving as if the two of them were alone. 'Try prayers. Go ahead with earlier plans.'

'Someone will tell him. You know they will. You know Hong Kong.'

'Oh, probably. If so, I suppose that'll be it. But I wonder? He doesn't sound the ordinary old blimp, your future husband.'

'What is all this?'

'It is something, Nick,' said Mrs Baxter, 'that I don't think we should be listening to. You are making us eavesdroppers, Amy.'

'I've more to do than stand here dropping eaves,' said Nick. 'I'm teaching a Moral Sciences seminar in twenty minutes.'

Amy and Elisabeth continued to stand in silence and it was (surprisingly) Amy who began to cry.

'You're – oh, if you knew how I envy you, Bets! You're so *innocent*. You're going to be so *ghastly* soon. All this will be an uneasy memory when you're opening bazaars around the Temple church in the Strand, and organising book groups for barristers' wives. You'll metamorphose into a perfect specimen of twentieth-century uxorial devotion. You'll have this one guilty secret, and you'll never forgive me for knowing.'

'I don't know what the hell's going on,' said Nick.

'You and I, Bets, will be the last generation to take seriously the concept of matrimonial fidelity. Wait until this lot get cracking with sex and sin in the – what? – in the Sixties.'

'How do you know?' said Elisabeth.

'I know.'

'Are you *happy* about it, Amy?'

'I am bloody, bloody *unhappy* about it. Have a child at your peril, Bets. It will hurt you to hell.'

One of the children then began to cry for its dinner and slap, bang went Amy with the rice pot.

'Nick – take Betty *now*. Bets, see you at the altar. Right?'

Mrs Baxter began to sing 'When I survey the wondrous Cross' as she unwrapped the wet child, who at once spread out its wet legs and went thankfully to sleep.

Chapter Eight

At last there was a message for Elisabeth Macintosh when she returned to the Old Colony Hotel. She was called over to the reception desk and an official-looking letter was put into her hands. The envelope came from Edward's London Chambers and it chilled her. Her name was typewritten. So, it was all over.

She took it upstairs – the bedroom still untouched, the two beds a mess, but she found a red light flashing by the telephone. Which first? Face the one you fear.

She opened the letter and inside, in Edward's beautiful, clear script, read, *I have wonderful news. Ross will bring you to the Old Repulse Bay Hotel tonight to celebrate it. I have not had a minute – literally, I mean it – to telephone or write. You will soon see why. I love and long for you, Edward.*

She contemplated the message light for a while and then rang down to reception. While they dialled up the message, she sat with the blunt, heavy block of the black receiver in her hand. At length, after much clicking, a voice, a recording from somewhere: *This is Mr Albert Ross, consulting solicitor to Mr Edward Feathers QC. I am to call for a Miss Elisabeth Macintosh this evening to take her to dinner with Mr Feathers and his team. The dress code will be formal. Six o'clock.*

Who is this pompous ass? The famous Loss the Demon Dwarf? So, we shall meet. I'm not going to like him. I'm being played with by all of them. I've half a mind . . .

And 'dress code formal'! What in hell? I've no money and nothing clean and Edward must – should – know it. As if he did!

She went to the waste-paper basket and fished out the dress.

No. I couldn't. I can never wear it again. It feels cold and wet. I can hardly bear to touch it. (But she held it to her face.)

I suppose I could get them to press it. Laundry service? But just touching it, looking at it, makes me want to cry. With happiness, private happiness, not with guilt. Once only. It is a sacred dress. And she pressed her face into it and remembered Veneering's hands and skin and hair and sweat as the dress lay like a slop of spinach on the wood floor of the weird tree house. I will never wear it again.

Time? It's still only two o'clock. I've over three hours. Food? Not hungry. Perhaps try. Get room service. Get a saté from a stall.

She turned in her cotton clothes into the poor streets again, stepping through litter and ordure. A man without legs sat, his crutches splayed, opening shellfish, the shells thrown about him. She bought a pork saté from a boy yelling 'Saté' insolently in her ear. Then she bought a warm, soft prawn fritter and stood eating it all. It smelled sweet and good. Looking up above the street stalls she saw on a hoarding a huge photograph. It was a young European girl naked to the waist and smelling a rose. It was, undoubtedly, Lizzie.

Well, of course not. How could it be? Lizzie was an intellectual. She'd been at Bletchley Park. And she was, or said she was, a lesbian. One didn't think about it. She was always coming and going to Hong Kong. She told you nothing. There were rumours of her having something to do with the Chief of Police. She had known some terrible people, even at school. But she'd been serious, hard-working. But naked to the waist and a rose! *Smelling* the rose! *Lizzie*! Well, she does say she's broke. No, I'm just tired.

I am wonderfully, deeply tired, and I want him again. And again. And for ever. And I don't mean Edward.

She wandered the street stalls, licking the prawn juice off her fingers. She peered into fragments of looking-glass, demons and cartoon toys. Wherever she went among the stalls were clusters of children eating where they stood, quietly, prodding their chopsticks into thimble dishes of fish and pork. Oh, how could I ever go West again? I'll stay here. With anyone who wants me. One or the other. With anyone.

She had shocked herself. She had meant it. She'd go

with a man who would let her roam in the market. 'I'll go down fast,' she told the poster. The girl with the rose now did not look like Lizzie at all. It was some American film star. Hedy Lamarr. She wondered how much the girl had been paid.

She was in the Old Col Hotel again. It was half past four in the afternoon. Make-up? Borrow Lizzie's. (God, I look tired.) Dress? Green dress. I forgot to get them to iron it. It smells and I don't care. I'll never, never own such a beautiful dress again. And nobody will ever know. He won't be there. Not at Edward's party with its 'wonderful news' – whatever that is.

When she was dressed she looked – after a little hesitation – out of her window and saw a white Mercedes parked outside, its windows dark and its number plate so short it looked like royalty.

'I shall certainly not hurry,' said the new Elisabeth and sauntered forth, her hair curly again, springy after the shower. I'm walking differently, she thought. They say you can always tell when a virgin is a thing of the past.

The car with the black windows gave no sign of remarking on her non-virginal condition, her walk, or on anything about her. When she stopped beside it nothing happened, and she felt snubbed. If there was a driver inside, he was invisible. This was not a car you could tap, or try a door handle. It might set off some terrible alarm.

The crowds were surging now from work. They parted around the Mercedes and then came back together again beyond it. Nobody looked at her or noticed her. As Nick had said this morning at the noisy family flat, 'You get lonely here, you know. It's not that they dislike you so much as that they aren't interested. They just blot you out. Just occasionally they make it plain. You can be sitting on a bus with the only empty seat the one beside you, and there'll be Chinese standing thick down the middle of the bus all down the centre aisle, and there'll never, ever, be one of them who will sit down beside you. We are invisible.'

Elisabeth, standing in her green dress by the car, now felt invisible. She decided to turn back. After all, I'm not just *anyone*. She would go back to the bedroom and wait to be taken properly to Edward's party. I am a grown woman.

And yet, I'm still telling myself stories. I have not had the courage to throw away childish things. You'd never take me for a linguist and a sociologist and an expert in ciphers, and all of it after being in the Camps. There is something missing in me. I'm empty.

Tears began to come. She knew that it was love that was missing. Edward was missing. She had forgotten all about him. Put him ruthlessly into memory.

'Good afternoon,' said someone behind her, and she looked down to see a very short, thickset troll of a man wearing a brown felt hat. He removed it.

'I am Albert Loss. I cannot say my "ahs". I am the instructing solicitor and almost lifetime friend of Mr Edward Feathers QC. I am instructed to drive you out to Repulse Bay to dine with him.'

A white-uniformed driver now stood beside the car's opened doors. She was put behind the driver and Ross next to her on a built-up seat that set them on a level. The air-conditioning after several minutes was cool and silent, and the car slid carefully through the crowds and away.

'You said something –' she turned to Ross. 'You said something like "QC". Edward is too young to be made a Queen's Counsel.'

'He has just been made one. I mentioned it in my telephone message.'

'No! *Has* he? I never took it in. Oh, how wonderful! He never told me he'd applied. Oh, I see! *Now* I see. This is to be a celebration.'

'Not altogether. He has other things to say. I shall leave the rest to him.'

'Oh, and he so deserves it. Oh, I hope he's letting himself be happy about it.'

'He will never let on,' said Ross, 'but he has been frequently smiling.' He removed his hat, turned it over, unzipped a small zip inside the crown and removed a pack of cards. He did up the zip again, dropped the hat to the floor and set up a little shelf. He began to deal himself a hand.

'I like cards, too,' she said. 'But will there be time? I thought we were almost there.'

'There is always time for cards and reflection. They are an aide-memoire. I am a compulsive player and I have a magnificent grasp of fact. My memory has been honed into an unbreakable machine. There is half an hour more of this short journey. We have to make a diversion on the way.'

'Won't Edward wonder? Worry?'

'He knows you are with me.'

'But where are we now?' She looked through the one-way glass window. 'You can't be driving a car like this up here.'

'It will take little harm. I agree that my London Royce would be more appropriate. And the card tray there is firmer.'

'But this is an awful place. Wherever are we going?'

Stretching away were building sites and ravaged land-scapes. Squalor and ugliness.

'It is your bread and butter – shall we say *our* bread and butter? And also our caviar. We are approaching the reser-voirs, the sources of legal disputes that will support us all for years to come. Off and on.'

'But it's horrible! It's a desecrated forest. It's being chopped down. Miles and miles of it.'

'There are miles more. Miles more scrub and trees. They will all, of course, have to go in time, which is sad since so much was brought here by the British. Like English roses in the Indian Raj, the trees here grew like weeds. It was once a very good address to have, up here, you know. The dachas of the British. I still have a small one here myself, just to rent out – here we are in the trees again – which I intend to sell. The area is not safe now after dark. The reservoir workers begin to frighten people.

They troop through the trees at sundown, like shadows. Here we are. My little investment.' And the car stopped in a glade on a mud patch where a dilapidated wooden box of a dwelling seemed to have become stuck up a tree.

'Oh, no!' she said. 'Oh, no – oh, no!'

The zigzag notice *Danger of Death* was in place at the foot of the ladder. The driver lifted Ross out of the car and locked the car again behind him and Elisabeth inside watched the little man unlock the gate, shuffle painfully up the ladder stair, unlock the front door and disappear. When he came out again the driver lifted him back to his seat, relocked the car doors.

Ross sat on his perch and said nothing.

'Can we go? Can we *please* go now?' she said. 'Please, I don't like it here, it's horrible.'

'I let it by the hour,' he said. 'Night or day. It has been a good investment.'

'It's disgusting. Vile. Please can we go to Edward? Tell him to start the car. Does Edward know you own this?'

'Certainly not. When I bought it, it was for myself. A haven of peace in my difficult life, watching the cards. But I have let things slide. I live in so many places. I let it, in a very discreet way. And I am getting rid of it now.'

'Yes. Please. Can we go?'

'On one condition,' said the dwarf. 'That you will never think of it or of any such place again.'

'Of course not. Of *course* not. Look, I'm feeling cold –'

'And that you will never leave Edward.'

'He knows. I've told him I'll never leave him. I swear it.'
'If you leave him,' said Ross, 'I will break you.'

At their destination the driver got out to open her door, and Ross tossed over to her a green silk purse.

'You left your passport behind,' he said.

Chapter Nine

She heard laughter. Cheerful shouting. English laughter, and across the terrace saw Eddie's legal team all drinking Tiger beer. There were six or seven of them in shirts and shorts, and Edward standing tall among them without a tie, head back, roaring with laughter. The cotton dress would have been right.

Edward came striding over to her, stopped before he reached her, held out a hand and took her round a corner of the terrace out of sight of the others. He looked young. He held her tight. He took both her hands and said, 'Did you think I'd forgotten you?'

'Yes.'

'Do you know what's happened?'

'Yes. You've got Silk. You're a QC.'

'No. Not that. Do you know that the Case has settled?'

'No!'

'It's taken sixteen hours. Sixteen solid hours. But we've settled out of court. Neither side went to bed. But everyone's happy and we can all go home. Ross is packing the papers.

The other side's off already. Veneering left this morning, so the air's pure again.'

'Eddie – you've all lost a fortune. *How* much a day was it? Thousands?'

'No idea,' he said, 'and no consequence. I've got the brief fee. It'll pay for the honeymoon. I've told Ross and the clerks to get it in, and then that I don't want any more work until I'm back in London. I've said two months. I've told him to give everything to Fiscal-Smith.'

'Whoever's that?'

'Someone who's always hanging about. Takes anything and pays for nothing. The meanest lawyer at the Bar. An old friend.'

She sat down on the parapet and looked across the sea. He hadn't asked her one thing about herself. Her own plans. He didn't even know whether she had a job she had to get back to. If she had any money. About when her holiday ended. She tried to remember whether he'd ever asked anything about her at all.

'We might go to India,' he said. 'D'you want a cup of coffee? You'll have had dinner somewhere, I hope.' He and the noisy group of liberated lawyers had dined very early. Final toasts were now going round. Taxis arrived. Farewells. More laughter. Edward and Elisabeth were alone again under the same stars as before. After a time she said, 'I'd like to stay in the hotel here tonight, Eddie. I love this place. And no, I haven't had dinner.'

'But we have our hotel rooms Kowloon-side. And haven't you the Australian friend? She'll wonder where you are. And I haven't a shirt up here. For tomorrow.'

'She's left for Home, tonight, I think. We only met up here. We're old friends. We take it lightly.'

She watched him.

'There's the wedding to plan.'

'Oh, yes,' she said. 'I keep forgetting. I suppose that's my job. By the way, I haven't any money at all.'

'Oh, I'll deal with that.'

'Not until I'm thirty. I'll be quite well off then.'

He smiled at her, not interested.

They hardly spoke on the ferry. At Kowloon the lights of the Peninsular Hotel blazed white across the forecourt. The Old Colony was lit down the side street with its chains of cheap lights and was resounding with wailing music and singing. It was still only nine o'clock.

'It's only nine o'clock,' she said. 'Goodnight then, since you say so,' and at last he seemed to come to himself.

'Yes. Nine. All out of focus. I'm sorry. Come in. Come in to the Pen and I'll give you dinner. We'll both have some champagne. Betty?'

She was staring at him. 'No,' she said. 'I'm going over to some friends in Kai Tak.'

'Kai Tak! Isn't that a bit off-piste?'

'Yes. So are they. They're missionaries. Hordes of kids. Normal people. In love with each other. My friends.'

'Elisabeth – what's wrong? It is *on*, isn't it?'

Sitting in the taxi she said, after a minute, 'Yes. It's on. But I need the taxi fare.'

'Shall I come with you?'

75

'No. I'll be staying the night. Maybe longer,' and she was gone.

She saw him standing, watching her taxi disappear, and then the hotel's white Mercedes roll along with all the legal team waving at him, making for the airport and Home. In very good spirits.

He was, in fact, unaware of them, but saying to himself that he'd made some mistake. Had made an absolute bloody bish. I wish Coleridge were here. I'm not good at pleasing this girl.

Betty, bowling along through the alleys round Kai Tak, was thinking: He's shattered. He looked so bewildered. He's so bloody good. Good, good, good.

Well, I'll probably go through with it. I'll be independent when I'm thirty. I'll probably put a lot into it. I'll damn well work, too. For myself. QC's wife or not. And at least I have a past now. No one can take that away.

Chapter Ten

Since the night of celebration at Repulse Bay and the end of the land reclamation Case and the horrible parting outside the Peninsular Hotel, Elisabeth had moved in with Amy at Kai Tak. It was at Amy's command.

'Have you room for me?'

'Yes. There's a camp bed. And don't be grateful, you'll be very useful. Take the baby – no, not that way. Now, stick the bottle in her mouth – go on. Right up to the edge. She won't choke, she'll go to sleep and we can talk before Nick comes in.'

The other children were already asleep. Mrs Baxter must at some point have been taken up to her barbed-wire fortress. The Buddhists were practising silence on the floor below.

'Now then,' said Amy. 'Date of wedding?'

'Edward's arranging everything. The licence. I expect I'll have to be there at some point for identification. In case he should turn up with someone different.'

'You're being flippant.'

'Not that he'd probably notice.'

'Now you're being cheap. Seriously, Elisabeth Macintosh – is it on? It is a Sacrament in the Christian Church.'

'I'm being told yes from somewhere. Probably only by my rational self. There's no way I will say no, yet I don't quite know why. Marriage will be gone in a hundred years in the Christian Church. There'll be women priests and homo priests. Pansies and bisexuals.'

'You're tired. You live alone. What does Isobel say?'

'She's disappeared. As she always did. She was never any help with people's troubles, was she? She just stared and pronounced – if she could be bothered. She's burdened with her own secrets, but she never lets on.'

'I suppose she must tell someone. Some wise and ageing woman with a deep, understanding voice. And a beard.'

Elisabeth laughed and said, 'Can I pull this teat out now? She's asleep.'

Nick came in. It was very late. Very hot.

Elisabeth, lying on the camp bed near the kitchen sink, listened to the clamour outside in the sweltering streets, the thundering muted lullaby of the mah-jong players in all the squats around.

'I have no aim,' she said. 'No certainty. I am a post-war invertebrate. I play mah-jong in my head year after year trying to find something I was born to do. I have settled on exactly what my mother would have wanted: a rich, safe, good husband and a pleasant life. All the things she must have thought in the Camp were gone for ever. Impossible for me, the scrawny child playing in the sand. Hearing screams, gunfire, silences in the night, watching lights searching in the barbed wire. I should be the last woman in the world to recreate the old world of the unswerving English wife. I am trying to please my dead mother. I always am.' She slept.

And woke to Mrs Baxter flopping about with teacups saying, 'I tried not to wake you. Are you staying long? Shall we say a prayer together?'

She and Elisabeth were alone, except for the baby whom Mrs Baxter ignored. Nick, Amy and the rest were already about the Colony and the nursery school and the clinics. The noise from the streets was less than in the night, and the monks below were still silent. The telephone rang and it was Edward.

'Found you at last. Are you safe?'

'Of course. I'm going shopping.'

'Shall I come?' He sounded afraid of the answer.

'No. Do I have to come and sign things?'

'Not yet. I'm organising it. I'm planning our trip. Oh – Pastry Willy wants us to dine with them tonight.'

'Can't,' she said. 'Sorry. Next week? I must earn my keep here.'

'As to that, are you all right for money?'

'Rolling in it,' she said.

'Unexpected expenses –? Wedding dress and presents for . . .'

'You're the one for presents. First, Eddie, to Amy. She needs them. Don't dare to give her money; she'll just put it into a savings account for the children. Look – I'm staying here. They're my family. Until the wedding.'

'Willy's wife will be upset.'

'No. I want to be married from Kai Tak with the planes all roaring overhead.'

'Can you – I mean. Darling,' ('Darling'! Progress?) 'is there anywhere to wash there? A bathroom. To get ready on the day?'

'No idea. I must get on. I have to clean the kitchen.'

'Shall I come over? I think I should.'

'It's a free and easy place. Don't come in spats.'

'What on earth are spats?'

'Oh, stuff it, Edward.'

Mrs Baxter, pale as a cobweb, had been listening at the kitchen table where she was doing something with needle and thread. 'Was that a conversation with your fiancé?'

'I suppose it was, Mrs Baxter.'

She was silent as Elisabeth scoured away at the scum in the rice pot, black outside, silver within. Huge and bulbous. The black and silver raised a sense of longing in Elisabeth, of memory and loss: the outdoor kitchen in Tiensin, the servants' shouting, the stink of drains and cesspits, the clouds of dust, the drab sunlight and her mother appearing at the veranda door. The amah would come and pick up little Elisabeth, wiping her face with a grey cloth. She saw her mother's plump arms open towards her as she stretched her own stubby ones up to her mother. They all laughed. Her mother had been a blonde. She had twirled around with glee, swinging her baby. The servants were scouring the rice pots until their silver linings shone.

'You are not looking happy, Elisabeth.'

'But of course I'm happy, Mrs Baxter.'

'I am not a happy woman, either. I believe that you and I are very much alike. I thought so as soon as I saw you. I thought, She is born to tears and wrong decisions and she will need the consolation of Jesus Christ.'

'You've got me wrong, Mrs Baxter. I was thinking of my mother who never stopped laughing. I was a baby. She was beautiful, loving and hardly ever went to church.'

'Died in the Camps, I hear? Well, I shall pray for you,' and she took out her handkerchief.

'Mrs Baxter. I am about to be married. I intend to be very happy. I'll discover no doubt if I need Jesus Christ. And in what form. If it is in the form of sex and married love, then Jesus is for me. But I haven't much hope.'

Mrs Baxter sat thoughtfully. Later in the day when the family were all home again, she still sat thoughtfully. When Amy said that it was time for her to be taken home she said, 'I was a bride once.'

'And I bet you looked lovely.'

'Yes, Amy, I did. I had a very good dress, and it has survived. Elisabeth could wear it.'

'Thank you, but I . . .'

'Yet I feel that I should like to buy her a new one. I know a dressmaker and his wife who can complete in three days including covered buttons down the back. I shall see to it all if you will draw me a pattern. I still have my wreath of orange blossom that went round my head, but it is rather flat and discoloured.'

81

'Oh – I'll get one made for her,' said Amy. 'It can be my present. And I'll get the shoes. Those green ones she has are the shoes of a whore.'

'What I *do* possess,' said Mrs Baxter, 'and it will be in perfect condition in a tin trunk against weevils, is a veil of Indian lace. It is patterned with birds and flowers. St Anne's lace – a little pun – my name is Anne – made by the nuns in Dacca in what was then Bengal. You shall wear it – no, you shall *have* it. What use is it to me but as a shroud?'

'Betty – you could keep it for the baby,' said Amy, and the baby hiccuped on yet another bottle, and the other children put rice in their hair.

'My wedding day', said Mrs Baxter, 'was on a green lawn at the High Commission in Dacca, and there were English roses.' She wept.

'Accept,' said Amy. 'Quick. For God's sake.'

'Thank you very much indeed,' said Elisabeth. 'I believe your veil will bring me happiness.'

'Oh, I shouldn't count on that,' said Mrs Baxter.

PART TWO:
Happiness

Chapter Eleven

When he was very old and had retired to the Dorset country-side in England, and Betty dead, Old Filth as he was always called now, reverentially and kindly, would walk most after-noons about the lanes carrying his walking stick with the Airedale's head, pausing at intervals to examine the blossom or the bluebell woods, or the berries or the holly bushes according to the season. The pauses were in part rests, but to a passer-by they looked like a man lost in wonder or medi-tation. A dear, ramrod-straight man of elegiac appearance. As he grew really old, the English countryside was some-times on these walks shot through for an instant by a random, almost metallic flash of unsought revelation.

One November day of black trees, brown streams blocked with sludge and dead leaves, skies grey as ashes, he found himself in his room at the Peninsular Hotel again, and it was his wedding day.

It was early, and he was looking down at the old harbour-front YMCA building, everything ablaze with white sunlight. The flash of memory, like an early picture show, was all in black and white. The carpet of his hotel room was black, like velvet, the curtains white silk, the armchairs white, the telephones white. In the bathroom the walls and ceiling were painted black, the towels and flowers were white. There lay on a black glass table near the door of the suite a white gardenia and he, Edward Feathers himself, only just taken Silk (QC), at all of eight a.m., ready dressed in European 'morning dress' and a shirt so white that it mocked its surroundings by looking blue.

All these years later, he saw himself. He had been standing gravely at the window wondering whether or not to telephone her.

Breakfast?

He had not ordered a cooked breakfast. It would seem hearty. Others no doubt would be sitting down in their suites to bacon and eggs on the round black glass table, napkin startlingly white. But for Edward – well. Perhaps a cup of coffee?

Should he ring his wife-to-be? Amy's number? His – his Elisabeth? But then the telephone shouted all over his room.

'Hello?'

'It's me,' said Elisabeth.

'I was going to telephone you.'

'It's supposed to be bad luck,' she said.

'No, it's bad luck for me to *see* you before the church. I was thinking of – er – saying, well – well, how to get there – well, don't get the time wrong. Will those missionaries get you there? Willy could fetch you.'

'I'll be there, Edward.'

'All set, then?'

'All set, Edward. Edward, are you OK? Are you happy?'

'Don't forget your passport. Tell them to throw your suitcase in the back. Oh, and don't forget . . .'

'What?'

A long silence, and he watched the seabirds leaning this way and that over the harbour.

'Don't forget . . . Elisabeth. Dear Betty. Even now – are you sure?'

There was the longest pause perhaps in the whole of Edward Feathers's professional life.

And then he heard her voice in mid-sentence, saying, 'It could be cold in the evenings. Have you packed a jersey?'

'My breakfast hasn't arrived yet. Then I have to pay the bill here. Are you dressed? I mean in all your finery?'

'No. I've a baby on my knee and Amy and everyone are shouting. But, Eddie, if you like we can still forget it.'

'I'll be there,' he said. Silence again for an aeon. 'I love you, Betty. Don't leave me.'

'Well, mind you turn up,' she said briskly. Too brightly. And put down the phone.

He had no recollection, in the Donhead lanes after Betty's death, of any of this, except his own immaculate figure standing at the window.

'I am not going,' said Bets, hand still on the phone. 'It's off.'

Amy planted a glass of brandy beside the bride's cornflakes. 'Come on. Get dressed. I've done the children. What's the matter?'

'What in *hell* am I doing?'

'The best thing you ever did in your life. Looking ahead at last. Here, I'll do your hair.'

Edward's luggage had already gone ahead to the airport. He paid his bill at the desk, the management far from effusive, since they'd expected him there for another two months. But they knew he would be back, and he tipped everyone correctly and shook hands all round. They walked with him to the glass doors and bowed and smiled, nobody saying a thing about his stiff collar and tailcoat so early in the morning. 'You don't need a car, sir? For the airport?' 'No, no. I'm going across to church first.' 'Ah – church. Ah.' The gardenia in his buttonhole could have been laminated plastic.

He set out to his wedding alone.

Briefly he thought of Albert Ross. Ross had vanished. Eddie had no best man.

Oh, well, you can marry without a best man. No one else he'd want. It was a glorious morning. He remembered his prep-school headmaster, Sir, reading Dickens aloud, and the effete Lord Verisoft walking sadly to his death in a duel on Wimbledon Common with all the birds singing and the sunlight in the trees.

'I am alone, too,' he said in his mind to Sir. 'I haven't even a Second to chat to on the way.'

He thought of the old friends missing. War. Distance. Amnesia. Family demands. 'I have married a wife and therefore I cannot come.' Oxford friends. Army friends. Pupils in his Chambers. Not one. Not one. Oh my *God*!

Walking towards the exquisite figure of Edward Feathers – well, not so much walking as shambling – was Fiscal-Smith.

From Paper Buildings, London EC4!

They both stopped walking.

Then Fiscal-Smith came rambling up, talking while still out of earshot. 'Good heavens! Old Filth! This hour in the morning! Gardenia! Haven't you been to bed? I'm just off the plane. Great Scot – what a surprise! Where are you going?'

'Just going to church.'

'Case settled, I hear. Bad luck. I'm here for the Reclamation North-east Mining Co. It hasn't a hope. Oh, well, excellent! Thought you'd be on the way Home.'

'No, not – not just at once.'

'*Church*, you said? I'd no idea it was Sunday. Jet lag. I'll walk there with you.'

'No, that's all right, Fiscal-Smith.'

'Glad to. Nothing to do. Need to walk after the plane. Should really have shaved and changed. I always travel now in these new T-shirt things. Feathers, you do look particularly smart.'

'Oh, I don't know . . .'

'Ah. Oh, yes. Of course. You've just got Silk. All-night party. Well done. You look pretty spry, though.'

'Thank you.'

'Well, *very* spry. Good God, Feathers, you look like *The Importance of Being Earnest*. Nine o'clock in the morning. What's going on?'

Eddie stopped and turned his back on St James's church. At that moment, from the belfry a merry bell began to ring. 'Private matter,' he said, and held out his hand. 'Goodbye, old chap. See you again.'

'There's a clergyman waving at you,' said Fiscal-Smith. 'Several people in bright dresses are round the church door. Smart hats. The padre – he's coming over. He looks anxious –'

'*Goodbye*, Fiscal-Smith.'

'*Hello*!' cried out the parson. 'We were getting worried. Organist's on "Sheep May Safely" third time. You are looking very fine, my dear fellow, if I may say so. Now then – best man? Delighted. At the risk of sounding less than original I have to ask if you have the ring?'

'Ring?'

'Wedding ring? Let me see it. Best man – by the way, my name is Yo. Yo Kong. I am to officiate. And you are?'

'Well, I'm called Fiscal-Smith. I've just arrived.'

'Well done, well done. Right on time. The ring.'

Fiscal-Smith stood in unaccustomed reverence, and Feathers gave one of his nervous roars and took a small box from his pocket.

'Very good. Splendid. Very good indeed. Now if you will accompany me, both of you, to the front pew on the right. The bride should be here in five minutes.'

'Bride?' said Fiscal-Smith out of a tight mouth.

'Yes,' said Eddie, staring up at the east window.

'Who the hell is she?'

'Betty Macintosh.'

'*Who?*'

'Decided to get on with it. Case settled. No time to contact a friend.'

'Friend?'

'Best man. Quite in order to go it alone.'

'Oh, I don't mind. If you'd told me I'd have shaved. And I dare say you'll be giving me a present. Usual thing.'

'Of course. And you won't mind giving presents to the bridesmaids?'

'*What?*'

'I take it they all want the same. A string of pearls,' and Eddie was suddenly transported with boyish joy and began to boom with laughter, just as the organ left off safely grazing sheep and thundered out the Wedding March.

The two men were hustled to their feet and arranged alongside the front pew. Fiscal-Smith was handed the ring box and dropped it, and began to crawl about looking down gratings. Edward's old headmaster, Sir, used to say, 'You don't find many things *funny*, Feathers. The sense of humour in some boys needs nourishment.' But this, on the wedding day that he had greeted as if going to his death, Eddie suddenly saw as deliriously dotty. He guffawed.

A rustle and a flurry and a gasp, and the bride stood alongside the groom, who looked down with a cheerful face maybe to wink at good old Betty and say, 'Hello – so you're here.' Instead his face froze in wonder. A girl he had never seen stood beside him in a cloud of lace and smelling of orchids. She carried lilies. She did not turn to look at him. The face, invisible under the veil, was in shadow.

He could sense the delight of the small congregation – must be Amy and her husband, and Mrs Baxter and some children and, oh yes, of course, Judge Pastry Willy and his wife Dulcie. Willy was 'giving Betty away'. How they were all singing! Singing their heads off: *From Greenland's icy mountains to India's coral strand.* (A paean to the Empire, he had always thought. Whoever had chosen it?)

Someone had put hymn books into the hands of the bride and groom and the best man in his coloured T-shirt who was singing louder than anyone with the book upside down. (You wouldn't have expected Fiscal-Smith to know any hymns by heart.) The bride was trilling away, too, reading the hymn book through the veil.

I don't know this girl, Eddie thought. I suppose it's Betty. It could be anyone. She's singing in tune rather well. I didn't know that Betty could sing. I don't really know anything about her. I wonder if some other men – other man – does? I don't know her tastes. I only know that terrible green dress. I don't know the colour of her eyes. Oh!

The bride had been told to lift her veil to make the promises and there to his relief was Betty in his pearls, and her eyes were bright hazel. And she was standing with her right foot on his left foot, and quite hurting him. They made the tremendous promises to each other, like automata, and he was told that he might now kiss her.

Tears in his eyes, he leaned towards Betty who leaned towards his ear after the small, obligatory kiss. 'Who on *earth* is the best man?' just as Fiscal-Smith dropped the now empty ring box for the second time and turned to check how many un-necklaced bridesmaids there were. And, for the first time that day, Fiscal-Smith smiled, on finding that there were none.

Chapter Twelve

Honeymoon Letters

Letter one: A letter from the bride to her friend Isobel Ingoldby, of no fixed address.

Dear Lizzie,

I'm writing with no real idea yet of where to send it. Perhaps to the Old Col, in case you left a forwarding address. Are you east or west? Back in Oz, forward to Notting Hill, or in pursuit of some passion in the Everglades or one of the Poles?

I've done it. Wore ancient veil belonging to old bird. A Missionary Bird once in Dacca all butterflies and flowers to cover my homely face and a new dress that was a present from her too, and shoes from Amy and flowers from Uncle Pastry who walked me down the aisle and handed me over. Antique idea, but rather amazing. Eddie gave a sort of hiccup as I drew up alongside. I gleamed at him through the lace and I could see that he was worried that I might be someone else. He likes all evidence to be in the open. When I came to lift the veil – as does God at death – he looked startled, then breathed out thankfully. I'd made an effort with the face and had my hair cut where the grandee expats used to go, one of them looking down at me from a benign photograph on the wall. Must be long dead, but somehow I know her. Could have been part of my childhood. Friend of Ma, I guess. Red nails, shiny lips like a geisha girl with kind eyes. She's going to be my icon. I shall grow old like her, *commanding* people and being a perfick lady, opening bazaars. I'll live in the past and try to improve it. You'll know me by my hat and gloves, and hymn book too, like the mission-ary who got eaten by the casso-wary in Tim-buk-tu . . . something-something hymn book too.

Well, I suppose I got eaten in HK at the church but I'm not unhappy, being digested, just a little shaken. I don't know if Eddie's happy – who does know about him? – but I'd say he isn't shaken at all. The only thing that worried him apart from my heavy disguise under the antique tablecloth was his best man. You'd think Eddie would have been ashamed of Fiscal-Smith, but he's loyal to friends. And he has some funny friends, like the Dwarf – who was nowhere to be seen – and now this battered scarecrow. He thinks my friends are funny too, citing the excellent Mrs Baxter who does nothing but cry.

And if he knew I know *you*, what then! Don't worry,

ducky. I'm not jealous of his memories or that you were *in flagrante delicto* (more jargon) once upon a time. 'Let it be our secret that I know you,' as your lesbian pals undoubtedly bleat.

I don't think you and Eddie'd have much to say to each other now, Lizzie, whatever you both got up to in the school hols before the war.

And I find I have everything to say to him morning, noon and night. Old Filth, as he is so charmingly called – I can't care for it – is full of surprises. And I do enjoy the way people *defer* to him. I am but a hole in the air but they run after him, bowing. And why I like this so much, Lizzie, is that he doesn't notice it. And he doesn't think it odd to have friends like Fiscal-Smith and the seven dwarfs. Well, only one dwarf to date, but you never know who will turn up next.

And he trusts me utterly, Lizzie. Never suspected a thing about you-know-what. And I've put it out of my mind. It was some sort of hypnosis. Terrifying! No, I never think about it. Of course, Eddie's a bit of an enigma himself, and it makes me pleased with our Enigma years at Bletchley Park. You and I know about silence. Not one of us spilled a bean, did we? And the fact that I'll never really crack Eddie in a way gives me a freedom, Lizzie. Oh, not to misbehave again, oh dear me, no, but to have an unassailable privacy within my own life equal to his. This *must* be how to make marriage work. I have been married three full days. I know.

We're in Shangri-La, Lizzie. It's called Bhutan, and way round the back of Everest. He organised it all between the Case settling and marrying me. That's what he was doing the two days he vanished in Hong Kong. First he fixed a plane to Delhi – no, first the wedding breakfast at the Restaurant Le Trou Normand where Amy tried to breastfeed at the table and Eddie and Fiscal-Smith looked up at the ceiling that was all hung with fishing nets with fake starfish trapped in them, like Brittany, and the manager removed her to an annexe.

'Off to Delhi now,' says groom to bride and 'Delhi? We're not going to *Delhi*. Not *Agra*? Not the Taj Mahal with all the tours?' says bride to groom. 'I've not seen the Taj Mahal, as it happens,' he says, 'but no, it's a stopover. I couldn't get much of a hotel, though.'

Nor was it. The tarts paraded the corridors and *used* our room when we were down at dinner (British Restaurant wartime standard) and Edward inspected the bedcovers and *roared*, and we slept in chairs and next day he refused to pay and confetti fell out of my pockets and the manager smirked. Bad start.

But *then* I experienced the superhuman power of the Great Man's fury. Heathcliff stand back. Result: somehow comes along an Embassy car and chauffeur to take us to the airport, no Taj Mahal but a silent journey with Eddie like Jove on his cloud. And the cloud gave way to mountains, and the mountains were the Himalayas, and then the mountains started to change and soften and a pale green, misty valley country began. Its architecture

97

of wood and stone and bright paint is like a pure and unworldly Vienna. Tall, huge blocks of apartments like palaces. Cotton prayer flags blow in clusters from every hilltop and street corner and everyone – children and grandpas and cripples and monks – give each prayer wheel a little shove as they pass.

And now we have reached a rest-house high above a valley where a green river thunders, foaming along between forests standing in the sky and luminous terraces of rice. At a meeting of waters stands a stupa. Even from up here its whiteness and purity hurt the eyes. High up here we listen to the thunderous waters and then, high above us again, are monasteries hidden in the peaks, and eagles.

We arrived yesterday on a country bus and we passed this stupa far below at the meeting of the rivers. It is like the huge snow-white breast of a giantess lying prone with a tower on top, like a tall white nipple. Reclining by the roadside on a wooden bridge was a human-sized creature examining its fingernails like a courtesan, not interested in us. Bus stops still. Driver cries, 'Look, look! It is a langur, the rare animal you see on our postage stamps!' and the langur langur-ously yawns, putting a paw over its mouth – I swear – and vanishes.

> I'd like to be a langur
> Sitting by a stupa
> Eating chips and bang-ur
> Wouldn't it be supa?

Now, in this Bhutanese rest-house, I am completely happy and I hope Eddie is. He spends hours sweeping the view with his binoculars and peace on his face. The walls of the rest-house are made of crimson felt hung inside heavy skins. The red felt flaps and groans in the wind. It is damp to the touch. Monks and monkish people shuffle about. The appearance of the management puts the Savoy Hotel to shame. They wear deep-blue woollen coats, the Scottish kilt, long woollen socks knitted in diamond patterns like the Highland Games and dazzle-white cuffs turned back over blue sleeves. The cuffs are a foot deep. There's a whiff of Bluecoat Boys and of Oliver Cromwell. Puritan? No. There must be a lot of sex about for the villages teem with children and (wait for it) all the government offices are painted with murals several storeys high, with giant *phalluses* (or *phalli*?) on which Eddie sometimes lets his binoculars rest and even faintly smiles.

So, it's all OK, Lizzie-Izz.

Love you. Love you for not being at the wedding. If Eddie knew I knew you and was writing he'd send his love, but I'd rather he didn't. I must keep hold of his love all to myself at least at first, until I understand it.

Dinner is served. Looks like langur fritters.

Your old school chum

Bets

(Letter stamped by Old Colonial Hotel, Hong Kong 'To await arrival' and eventually thrown away.)

Two: A letter from the bride to her friend Amy of Kai Tak.

Amy, my duck, I'm writing from Dacca in East Pakistan but when I write to The Baxter (next one), I'll call it Bengal and I have to say that Bengal suits it better, even sans Lancers. The climate remains the same. Every other change political and historical is on the surface. I can't remember if you and Nick worked here? Actually you can't see much surface for most of it is water. It is hardly 'a land', but part of the globe where the sea is shallow and the sinuous silky people are almost fish but with great white smiling teeth. The 'lone and level land' stretches far away and the crowds blacken it like dust drifting. Nowhere in the world more different than the last place, i.e. the first call in our Honeymoon Progress which is becoming *global* and all arranged in secret and string-pulling by Eddie.

First, Bhutan. We were dizzy there, not with releasing passions, but with altitude sickness. We were level with the eagles. There was also a bit of food poisoning. I managed not to buy the goat's cheese they sell on the mountainside like dollops of soft cream snowballs set on leaves. 'You would last one hour,' says my lord. In the rest-houses the food came before us on silver dishes and looked ceremoniously beautiful: mounds of rice with little coloured bits of meat and fish and vegetables in it, warmish and wet, and only after a terrible day and night did we realise that anything left over is mixed in with the new stuff next day. Tourists are few. Probably mostly dead. The king hates tourists and you usually have to wait a year. Eddie was at Oxford with him after the war, and I was all for dropping in our cards in the hope of getting some Oxford marmalade and Christ Church claret. Eddie said no. Eddie is . . . but later.

First, beloved Amy, thank you from all parts of me for all you did for me and the speed at which you did it. I *hope* you liked Edward? He is monosyllabic in a crowd. He very much liked you and Nick, and was full of admiration for you controlling and producing a family among the poor and needy and weak in the head. He never mentioned your children, which is a bit frightening. He doesn't know I want ten – plus a nanny and several nursemaids and a nursery floor at the top of a grand house in Chelsea on the river. I can't help it. I read too many Victorian children's books of Ma's in China. And I miss my Ma. But don't worry. I'll probably be marching against the Bomb, unwashed and hugely pregnant like the rest.

Eddie couldn't believe you have always been my best friend ever. He thought you'd be pony club and debutanting and hot stuff on the marriage market. 'She was,' I said. Do you find that much-travelled men are the most insular? Like Robinson Crusoe? If he hadn't got stuck on that island, Robinson Crusoe'd have got stuck on another. Of his own making.

I'm writing myself into a mood to say real things to you, and maybe I should now quickly write myself out of it. Do you remember that book about marriage (Bowen?) that talks about the glass screen that comes down between a newly-wed couple and all their former friends? I'm not going to let this happen but I can see, after that terrifying 1662 marriage service, that it can eat into one. Well, it was you made me go through with it. Said I was at last being practical. I wasn't sure that you still thought so when you met Eddie, and I wish he hadn't stared so steadily and so high above your head.

Loyalty. And so I'll only say that we had a ghastly first night in Delhi, propped up in basket chairs because harlots had been using our beds. Then we went in a solid car (called 'An Ambassador') up the Himalayas to Darjeeling, where we were greeted by old English types and cold mutton and rice pudding and porridge, and our own room looking directly at dawn over the Katmanjunga. The occasional English flag. There was early-morning tea and everything perfect between white, white linen sheets. In the middle of the night Eddie said, 'I can't apologise enough,' which I thought weird after his spectacular performances. 'About the Delhi hotel,' he said.

There was some ghastly hang-up in his childhood. I don't want to know about it. I'd guess half the men with his background are the same. Well, he was so happy in the mountains.

Then after Bhutan we came on here to Dacca.

I've seen a chair in a dark shop. It is rose-and-gold, a

patterned throne from some old rajah's palace, but all tattered. I longed. I yearned. Eddie said, 'But we haven't a home yet.' This had not occurred to me. 'We could send it to Amy at first.' He looked at me and said, 'She wouldn't thank you.' You and I aren't very good at domiciliary arrangements, Amy. You leave yours to God and I'm still imprisoned by the past, and expect it to come again. It won't, any more than sherbet fountains. It's to be 'Utility furniture' now, for ever. I said, 'Sorry.' And he said, 'Hold on,' and he went into the back of the dark shop and came out saying, 'I've bought it. It can go to Chambers.'

And this, not the great rope of pearls he gave me, and not the ring and that, not the moment he saw me in the Baxter butterflies, was *the* moment. Well, I suppose when I knew I loved him.

I'll write to the Baxter next, and explain about leaving the veil behind. In twenty years I'll come to your little girls' weddings. During the twenty years I'll have been endlessly breastfeeding in the rose-red chair, and anywhere else I choose. Times will have changed. Maybe we'll be having babies on bottles? Or in bottles? Maybe men will be extinct too.

But women will always have each other. You gave me *such* a wedding.

Love to Nick and the babes – by the way, has the new one come? Don't let Baxter tears fall on its sweet head but give it a X from

Betty

Three: A picture postcard from the bride to Mrs Hildegarde Maisie Annie Baxter of Mimosa Cottage, Hai Tak, Hong Kong.

Dear Mrs Baxter,

This is only a note until I get home when I'll write to thank you properly for the veil. I have left it for the time being with Amy, but I think you should see it back in its box. I fear for it among the hordes in Sunset Buildings. It *made* the wedding.

I am sure we'll meet again, and I'm so glad you could come to the restaurant though I'm sorry about the bouillabaisse.

With love from Betty *Feathers*

(Card discovered unposted fifty years on in the Donheads down the cushions of a great red chair.)

Four: A letter from the bride to Judge Sir William Pastry of Hong Kong, posted in Valetta, Malta.

Valetta, Malta

Dear Uncle Willy,

We are up at 'Mabel's Place' and I don't think I have to explain that it's the medieval palace of the great Mabel Strickland on the hilltop and the blue sea all around. The walls must be six feet thick and inside there are miles of tall and shadowy stone passages, slit windows *for arrers*, no furniture except the occasional dusty carpet woven when Penelope was a girl, massy candelabra standing on massy oak chests. Our bed could be rented out in London as a dwelling: four posts, painted heraldry, old plumes drooping thick with dust, thick bedlinen like altar cloths. Wow!

But I expect you've been here lots of times. One day you'll make a wonderful governor of Malta, and they'd love you as much as they love Mabel in her darned stockings and tweed skirts. If you won't do it then I'd push Edward for governor instead. We'd bring up our ten children here and become passionate about the Maltese, and have picnics on the beach (the Maltese perched on chairs and making lace) and watch the British flag going up and down with the sun. Until it's folded up and put away.

But you won't even think of it. Are you still wanting Thomas Hardy and Dorset? I can't think why. Dorset sounds stuffy – full of people like us – and Malta is cheerful, flashing with the light of the sea. And they still *like* us here and we like them. That will become rare. Quite soon, Edward thinks.

But at present Grand Harbour is alive with British ships hooting and tooting, and the streets are alive with British tars and all the girls roll their black eyes at them on their way to Mass, which seems to take place every half-hour. Their mothers, believe it or not, still stride the corkscrew streets in flowing black, their heads draped in black veiling arranged over tea trays. Oh – and flowers everywhere, Uncle W! Such flowers!

It's been terribly bombed, of course, and it's pretty

filthy. Sliema Creek is covered by a heavy carpet of scum. The Royal Navy swims in it, though the locals tell them not to. It's the main sewer. They wag their heads. There's a rumour of bubonic plague, and yesterday a big black rat ran across Mabel's roses not looking at all well.

Of course the food is terrible, as ever it was. It was we who taught them Mrs Beeton's mashed potato! There is not much in the way of wine. *But* the wonderful broken architecture from before the Flood stretches everywhere: hundreds of scattered broken villages – Africa-ish – the occasional rose-pink palace decorated like a birthday cake. There are about a hundred thousand churches, bells clanking all day long and half the night. Dust inside them hangs as if in water, incense burns and the roofs (because of the war) are mostly open to the sky.

There is a passion for building here, and they're all at it with ropes and pulleys. Restoring and starting anew. It would be wonderful for Eddie's practice: plenty of materials. Malta is one big rock of ages cleft for us. It is full of cracks, and overnight the cracks fill with dew and flowers. The smell of the night-scented stocks floats far out to sea.

(Scene: Hong Kong
Willy's Dulcie: You aren't *still* reading Betty's letter!
Willy: She grows verbose. Don't like the sound of it.)

It will remain a mystery that the island never fell to the enemy. It was dive-bombed night and day, the people hiding deep in caves and (I gather) quarrelling incessantly and threatening each other's authority most of the time. There was almost a revolution. Then, in limped the battered British convoys with flour and meat and oil and sugar, and the pipes all playing and the cliffs black with cheering crowds.

(Willy: Now its military history. She's holding back.
Dulcie: She's going to be a British blimp in middle
             age if she's not careful. What about the
             honeymoon?
Willy: I think she's coming to that.)

We arrived here by sea from Rome. We flew to Rome from East Pakistan, and we arrived in East Pakistan from Bhutan! I think we were the only tourists. The king of Bhutan is pretty insular but he let us in because he was at Christ Church with Eddie. Not that they met. Then or then. He's an insular king – like you and Thomas Hardy. And maybe George VI.

London tomorrow. We'll be in Eddie's old London pad until we can find somewhere else. The Temple's bombed to bits still. I think – but don't spread it – that Eddie wants to come back to live in Hong Kong, and so do I, especially if you and Dulcie stay. Don't be lured back to the dreary Donheads.

I'm sorry. I run on with no means of stopping – Oh, God – History!

(Willy: I think she's stopping.
Dulcie: You'll be late for Court.)

I have so much to tell you, my dear godfather I've
known since Old Shanghai. This was to have been a
simple letter of thanks. Thanks for being such a prop
and stay at the wedding, for giving me away, for being
so diplomatic at Le Trou Normand about Amy
breastfeeding (tell Dulcie sorry about that, I didn't know
it would upset her) and especially when Mrs Baxter was
sick. You were wonderful. I'm afraid my Edward kept a
seat near the back! He was silent for a long time, but as
we passed through Sikkim en route for Darjeeling and
we saw slender ladies plucking tea leaves with the very
tips of their fingers – their saris like poppies in the
green, their little heads bound round with colours and I
was transported with joy – he said, 'I am not enough for
you.'

Oh dear – I have been carried far away. Please, dear
Uncle W, don't show Dulcie this. Well, I expect you will.

In Dacca Eddie bought me a red chair. The old, old
man who sold it lived far down the back of his shop in
the dark, his eyes gleaming like a Maltese plague rat.
The chair is to be sent to the Inns of Court, The Temple,
London EC4!

Oh – I don't seem to be able to concentrate on
thanking you. If only Ma and Pa were here. 'You are my
mother and my father,' as the Old Raj promised India,
or rather they said, 'I am.'

Isn't it odd how Hong Kong holds us still? Isn't it odd how the 'Far East' has somehow faded away with the Bomb? Do you understand? Now the British live out there by grace. I shall call my first daughter Grace.

I promise, dear Uncle Willy, to grow more sage: more worthy of your affection. I shall grow tweedy and stout and hairy, with moles on my chin, and I shall be a magistrate and open bazaars in support of the Barristers' Benevolent Society. You won't be ashamed of me.

Thanks for liking Eddie, with much, much love from Betty x

(Letter left in Judge Pastry's Will to Her Majesty's Judge Sir Edward Feathers QC, residing in the Donheads, carefully dated and inscribed and packed in a cellophane envelope, and bequeathed to Edward Feathers's Chambers where it may still be mouldering.)

Chapter Thirteen

'You are grinning all over your face, Mrs Feathers.'

'I'm happy, Mr Feathers. I'm writing to Pastry Willy.'

'About a hundred pages, at a guess. Come on. It's a picnic.'

'Picnic?'

'On the cliffs, Elisabeth. With the local talent. Well, the local English talent. Quick. No "PS xx". Envelope, stamp and off. Silver salver at the portcullis. Take your suncream and I've got your hat.'

'I love you, Edward Feathers. Why are we going off on a picnic with all these terrible people? We could be eating tinned pilchards with Mabel.'

'It'll be tinned-pilchard sandwiches on the cliffs. Come on, there's a great swarm going. Planned for years. Since the end of the war. It's all expats with no money, no education and big ideas. All drunk with sunlight. They drifted to Malta. They can't go home. Nothing to do.'

'Is it the British Council?'

'Certainly not. It's the riff-raff of Europe. The Sixpenny Settlers. We have to go. It's polite. There's to be wine.'

They arrived at the picnic where everyone was lolling about in the sun on what seemed to be an inland clifftop, though you could hear the sea far below. There was a long fissure on the plateau, stuffed full of flowers. There was a trickling sound of running water.

'I thought there were no streams on Malta,' she said.

'There is one. Only one,' said a languid man lying about nearby with a bottle of wine.

'We found it a year ago. Nobody knew of it. Yet it's no distance from Valetta,' said somebody else.

'Ah,' (the languid man). 'We find that the island gets bigger and bigger.'

Some daughters, English schoolgirls in bathing dresses, neat round the thighs, were laughing and jumping over the rift in the rock. And then a shriek.

'What's happening? What's happening, Eddie?'

'I think they're jumping the crack.'

Elisabeth ran across and lay on her stomach and looked down into the slit rock and its channel of flowers. It was less than a yard wide. The spot of emerald ocean below seemed as distant as the sky above. 'Oh, if they slip! If they slip!' Betty yelled out.

But the girls' mothers were sitting smoking and examining their nails, and one of them called, 'They won't. Don't worry.'

Then one girl did. A leg went down and she had to be

hauled out fast. Everyone laughed, except Elisabeth, who again lay face down. There was the notion that there was no time, nor ever had been, nor ever would be. She said, 'Eddie, there's a little beach down there. I can see breakers. I'm going down by the path.'

'If there is a path.'

'I'll find one. I'll go alone. Don't follow me.'

They had not been apart since the wedding.

The languid man lying near with his wine bottle called out, 'I say, you're the barrister chap, aren't you? I want to ask you something.'

'I'm off. I'll see you down there, Edward. Come for me in one of the cars. Don't hurry.'

'You'll miss the picnic.'

'Good. Don't drink too much. The road down will be screwy. Might be safer to dive through the crack.'

Edward turned grey. He strode over and grabbed her arm above the elbow.

'Let go! Stop it! You're like a tourniquet! *Edward*!'

His eyes were looking at someone she had never met.

Then he let go of her arm, sat down on the stony cliff and put his hands over his face. 'Sorry.'

'I should think so.'

'I went back somewhere. I was about eight.'

'*Eight?*'

'I killed someone –'

'Oh, Eddie, shut up. I'm going . . . No, all right, then. All *right*. I won't. Go and talk to that awful man. I'll sit here by myself.'

'Something wrong?' the man called. 'Honeymoon over? Something I said?'

'No,' said Edward.

'The war,' said the man. 'PoW, were you?'

'No. Were you?'

'God, no. Navy. Shore job. Ulcer. Left me low. Wife left too, thank God. Look.' He heaved himself up and came over to Edward. 'Can you get me a job? In the Law line? Something like barristers' clerk. No exams. Something easy.'

'Barristers' clerks don't have easy lives.'

'I'd really like just to stay here. On Malta. Do nothing. Just stay with our own sort.'

'I can't stand this,' said Elisabeth. 'Eddie, come with me down the cliff.' She stepped over the man and said, 'Oh, drop dead, whoever you are.'

Chapter Fourteen

The streets around Victoria Station were dark, and the taxi crawled along in a fog so dense that kerb-stones were invisible and even double-decker buses were upon you before you knew it. The cab driver stopped and started, and they sat silent until he said at last, 'Ebury Street. Yes? Ten pounds.' He had brought them all the way from the airport, their luggage piled around them and under a strap on the front and on top on a frame. 'Thanks, sir. Good luck, sir.'

She had never seen Edward's part of London. She had never seen him in a house at all. Always it had been hotels and restaurants. She had no idea what his maisonette in Pimlico would be like, and still less now they had drawn up outside it in thick fog. She had always been with him in sunlight.

'I should carry you over my doorstep,' he said, 'but it's going to be a bit cluttered,' and he unlocked the front door upon an unpainted, uncarpeted stairwell with the yellow gloaming of the fog seeping in through a back window.

There was an untrampled mess of mail about the floor-boards and the smell of cats and an old-fashioned bicycle. Uncarpeted stairs went up and round a corner into more shadow.

'Home,' said Edward.

'Whose is the bike?'

'Mine.'

'*Yours*? *Can* you? I mean, I can't see you riding a bike.'

'I ride it every Sunday morning. Piccadilly. Oxford Circus. Not a thing on the road. I'll get you one.'

Upstairs there was a kitchen that housed one chipped enamel-topped table and a chair. Under the table were old copies of the *Financial Times* and the *Daily Telegraph* so densely packed that the table legs were rising from the floor. A rusty geyser hung crooked over a Belfast stone sink. Cupboard doors hung open against a wall. On the table, green fish-paste stood in an open glass jar and a teacup from some unspecified time. It had a mahogany-coloured tide-mark inside it.

Edward smiled about him. 'I have a cleaner, but it doesn't look as if she's been in. I've never actually met her. I leave the money by the sink and it disappears – yes, it's gone, so I suppose she's been. I hope the bed's made up. I'm not good at all this. I'm hardly ever here. There's a laundry round the corner and an ABC for bread.'

'You *live* here! All the time? Alone? But Eddie, it's so *unlike* you.'

'Oh, I don't know. I've never been fussy.'

There was a Victorian clothes airer attached to the ceiling

on a pulley with ropes that brought it up and down. Sitting on one of the rails of the airer was a rat.

Over the years, this homecoming became one of Elisabeth's famous stories, as she sat in Hong Kong at her rosewood dining table with its orchids and silver and transparent china bowls of soup. Contemporaries discussing post-war London. Elisabeth became glib, inspiring like memories among guests who were all of a certain age. They joked proudly of the drabness of that Fifties – even Sixties – London; the insanity of the National Health Service ('free *elastoplast*!'), the puritanical government. Elisabeth, always pleasant, never joined in about politics. She revered the British Health Service, and turned the conversation to the London she came to as a bride, to Edward's unworldliness in seedy Pimlico, his hard work, his long hours in Chambers. But when she told the homecoming story, which became more colourful with the years, she could not decide why she somehow could never include the rat.

She had screamed, run from the kitchen, down the stairs and out into the fog, and stood shaking on the pavement, Edward following her and shouting, 'Betty – for God's sake, there were rats on Malta. *Plague* rats. And Hong Kong. And what about Bhutan, and the snakes coming up the bath pipes?'

'We never saw one.'

'What about the Camp in Shanghai?'

'That was different. And we kept the place clean. We've got to leave, Eddie. *Now*.'

'You don't know how hard it is to find anywhere. Even one room. Everywhere is flattened. And Ebury Street is SW1. It's a good address on writing paper.'

'That rat wasn't there to write letters!'

Forty or so years on, in Dorset in her Lavendo-polished house and weedless garden, driving her car weekly to the car wash, refusing to keep a dog because of mud on its paws, a blast of memory sometimes overcame her. There sat the rat on the airer. It was her falling point. It was the rat eternal. It had been the sign that she must now take charge.

'Isn't there a hotel? Isn't the Grosvenor around here? At Victoria Station? We'll get the luggage back on the pavement and go there in a cab.'

'We'd never get another taxi in this fog,' he said, and at once a taxi swam out of the night, its headlamps as comforting as Florence Nightingale.

'I'm not sure if I've any English money left,' he said.

'I have,' she said. 'I bought some at the airport. Slam the front door behind you.'

She climbed in, and after a moment he followed.

And at Grosvenor Place they were out, they were in the foyer and the cabman paid off while Edward still stood frowning on the pavement in his linen suit. 'This hotel smells. It smells of beer and tobacco and fry. It's probably full up.' But she secured a room.

In bed he said, 'I always rather liked rats.'

That night in the Grosvenor in an unheated bedroom, shunting steam trains clamouring below, yellow fingers of fog painting the window and a mat from the floor on top of the skimpy eiderdown, Edward began to laugh. 'I am the *rat*,' he said, grabbing her. 'I came with you in the taxi.'

Scene in HK. Rosewood dining table. In middle age.
Fin de Siècle.

Edward (*to guests*): End of my freedom, you know. Minute we reached London, she took me over. She and the clerk and, of course, Albert Ross. Needn't have existed outside work.

All: Well, you *did* work, Filth! How you worked!

Edward: Yes. Work at last began to come in. Remember, Betty?

Elisabeth: I do.

Edward: Don't know what you did with yourself in the evenings, poor child. You looked about sixteen. All alone.

Elisabeth: Not exactly.

Chapter Fifteen

By the morning the fog had lifted and Edward was off to Chambers with his laundry and papers by nine o'clock. Across the table of the gloomy breakfast room at the Grosvenor Hotel, he handed Elisabeth the keys of the maisonette.

As soon as he'd gone she picked up the keys, asked for the luggage to be brought down and taken round to the station left-luggage office. She paid the bill and set off on foot, bravely, to Edward's horrible domain.

As she reached the corner of Ebury Street the fog rolled away and she saw that Edward's side of the street was beautiful in morning light. The façade was faded and gentle and seemed like paper, an unfinished film set, almost bending in the wind. The eighteenth-century windows that had withstood the bomb blasts all around were unwashed, yet clear, set in narrow panes. Little shops on to the pavement ran all along, and doors to the houses above had rounded fanlights. Each house had three storeys. There were two tall first-floor windows side by side with pretty iron balconies. The shop at street level beside Edward's front door seemed to be a greengrocer's, with boxes and sacks spread about the pavement and a very fat short man in a buff overall was standing, hands in pockets, on the step. 'Morning,' he said, blowing air out of his cheeks and looking at the sky.

'Are you open yet? Have you – anything?'

'*Anything*? I'd not say *any*thing. We have potatoes. Carrots. Celery, if required.'

'Have you – apples?'

He looked at her intently and said, 'We might have an orange or two.'

'Oh! Could I have two pounds?'

'Where you been then, miss? I'll sell you one orange.'

She followed him inside the shop where a doom-laden woman was perched high on a stool behind a desk.

'Look at my ankles,' she said, sticking one out. It bulged purple over the rim of a man's carpet slipper, unstockinged. 'D'you want a guess at the size of it?'

'It looks horribly swollen,' said Elisabeth.

'It's sixteen inches round. Sixteen! And all water. That's your National Health Service for you.'

'But you must go to the doctor at once.'

'And who does the accounts here? You reached home, then?'

'Home?'

'Next door. "Mr Feathers is home," they said, the electrician's across the road. Mozart Electrics.'

'We're – we're just passing through. I'm Mrs Feathers.'

'Well!' She rolled her eyes at her impassive husband, who was again on the step cornering the market. 'Married!'

'You can have two,' he called over his shoulder. 'But don't ask for lemons.'

'Sack that cleaner,' said his wife. 'She stays ten minutes. You'll have to get scrubbing.'

'Oh, well. I don't think we're staying. We want to get something nearer the City.'

'You'll be lucky,' said the woman. 'But you are lucky, I can see that. There'd be a thousand after next door the minute you handed in the keys.'

'I saw a rat. Last night. We left.'

'Oh, rats. They're all over the place, rats. Mr Feathers used to complain sometimes, though he's a perfect gentleman. "Have you by any chance got a dog, Mrs – er?" (he calls everyone Mrs – er). "Does your dog like rats?" We said we didn't know, but we took it round and it stands there looking at this rat' – a huge wheezing and shaking soon taken up by the greengrocer on the step, the rolls of fat beneath the buff vibrating – 'and it turns and walks out. The dog walks out. It was a big rat.'

'Well, I can't live here,' said Elisabeth.

'I'll get you the Corporation,' said the wife. 'You'll be clean and sweet there soon, you'll see. D'you want some kippers?'

Elisabeth turned the key in Edward's lock and then stood back for a while on the pavement, watching the electrical shop across the road opening up. A very arthritic old person stood watching her.

'Go on in,' he called. 'You'll be all right. 'Ere, I'll come in with you,' and like one risen painfully from the dead he slowly crossed the road, cars stopping for him. 'Takes me over an hour now to get up in the morning,' he said. 'Now watch that bike. The stairs is steep but if I take it slow . . . I'se easing. Now then . . .'

In the kitchen the airer was unoccupied, and through a beautiful window, its glazing bars as fine as spars, lay a long, green, tangled garden full of flowers. Upstairs and upstairs again were bedrooms with tipping floors and simple marble fireplaces. Edward's narrow bed stood like a monk's pallet in the middle of one room, on a mat. One fine old wardrobe. One upright chair. A decent bathroom led off, and now the higher view showed a row of other gardens on either side. On the other side from the green grass was a small lawn and forest trees blocking out Victoria Station's engine sheds.

'Don't you get too far in with her next door that side,' said the electrician. 'I don't mean Florrie with the ankles. I mean t'other side. You all a'right now?'

'Yes. Well. I shan't be staying. We saw – well – rats.'

'From the river,' he said. 'They have to go somewhere. There's worse than rats. Now, this is a good house and so it should be. We hear it's two pound a week rent. Mind, it's all coming down for development soon. Miracle is that not a bomb touched it. All the big stuff came down – Eaton Square and so on – not a window broken here. Artisans' dwellings, we are. But panelling original pine. I'll leave you for the moment.'

'Thank you,' she called down after him. 'Very much. Could you tell me why you're called Mozart Electrics?'

'Well, he was here as a boy,' said the arthritic, amazed that the whole world did not know. 'One day there'll be a statue.'

She found her way to the garden and there were fruit bushes and a cucumber frame, and over the fence to the right an old woman with a florid face was watching her.

'Good morning,' she said. 'I am De-lilah Dexter. You may have heard of me. I am an actress, but equally concerned with gardening. And I hear that you have just married Edward.'

'How ever –?'

'News flies through eighteenth-century walls. We heard you arrive last night, but then you were gone. I suppose he's off to his Chambers?'

'Yes. We're just back –'

'From a long honeymoon. It will be hard to adjust. I suggest you come in for hot cocoa and to meet Dexter.'

'I don't think . . .'

'I will put on the cocoa and leave open the front door.'

'This,' Delilah said, pointing, 'is Dexter.'

The house was like the green room of a small theatre, the sitting room apparently immense since the wall opposite the windows (hung with roped-back velvet like proscenium arches) was covered by a gold-framed mirror that reflected an older, softer light than was real. The mirror had a golden flambeau at either side of the frame where fat wax candles had burned to the last inch. The looking-glass reflected a collapsed man in a black suit, his legs stretched out before him on a red velvet chaise longue that lacked a leg. His face was ivory. He waved an exhausted greeting.

'Dexter', announced his wife, 'is also an actor. A fine actor, but in his later years he only plays butlers.'

'How interesting . . .'

'Butlers have been our support for years. Unfortunately the new drama is uninterested in butlers. It is all tramps and working-class women doing the ironing. But still, here and there Dexter finds a part, or rather directors find a part for him. He's the ultimate butler. He very much favours the Playhouse, where they still tend towards the country-house comedy, and long runs. At present he is in a play where his part ends with Act Two, and so he gets home for supper. They let him off the final curtain.'

'I hope always to be let off the final curtain,' said Dexter. 'And as I always wear black I need spend no time in the dressing room. I can leave this house and be on stage in nine minutes.'

'But if you fell over in the street?'

Both actors looked at Elisabeth with disdain.

'We are professionals,' said Delilah. 'We can dance on a broken leg. If Dexter *should* get late, he could borrow Edward's bicycle. I'll top up your cocoa with a little green chartreuse.'

When Elisabeth had opened every window in the house and propped open the front door with the bicycle, she followed Edward's telephone wire under a cushion and phoned the

Westminster Council about the rat. Then she got busy with the labour exchange and went across to Mozart Electrics about a cleaning agency. At the National Provincial Bank on the corner she opened an account, and she attacked the gas showrooms to dare them not to replace the geyser. 'They'll not show up for a month,' said Delilah Dexter, but someone came round in an hour and stayed until hot water crept forth. Elisabeth found a saucepan, cleaned out spiders and ate kippers.

'They were very good,' she told the greengrocer's wife.

'Yes, They're from Lowestoft. These are Lowestoft kippers – we've gone there two weeks' holiday for twenty-seven years, even in the war. You'll be all right, they keep. We'll be back there in a few months and I'll get you some more. We don't like change. We're here.'

Edward, returning uneasily – and late – that evening to the Grosvenor, found no sign of his wife or his luggage. He walked back dispiritedly to Ebury Street to find every light in the house ablaze, every window open and a smell of kippers noticeable as far away as Victoria Station. His wife on his doorstep, arms akimbo in a borrowed overall, was deep in conversation with the fruit shop, and Mr Dexter was making his way solemnly down the street dressed as a butler.

'The end of Act Two,' said Dexter, raising his bowler hat.

PART THREE:
Life

Chapter Sixteen

'Well, yes. There is money,' Edward agreed. 'Yes.' (Reluctantly.) 'The fees do begin to roll in at last. But I feel we should not be rash.'

'Decorate white throughout,' said Betty. 'The electric shop knows a couple of men down the mews. Then the new place, Peter Jones in Sloane Square, it's reopened. It's the place for all carpets and curtains. And furniture. Do you think it's time we had a car?'

'Good God, no!'

'It could stand in the road.'

'It would need lights at night.'

'We could have a wire through the sitting-room window. On a battery. They all do.'

'It's against the law. It's carrying a cable across the public highway. One day the whole street will catch fire.'

'The fruit shop van stands outside all the time. By the way, he says he'll deliver free.'

'Since he's only next door . . .'

'And Delilah Dexter's going to help me with the interior decoration.'

'Which one is Delilah Dexter?'

'Married to the singing butler. They know you. Leave it all to me, but I need a bank account of my own. And something to put in it.'

'That', said Filth, 'is, I imagine, usual now.'

Delilah was very decisive when the bank account was in place. The whole house was to be the very purest white, like Lady Diana Cooper's used to be in the Thirties, though she wasn't, Delilah found, the purest white herself. Nor was England. 'And we'll have one sitting-room wall in simulated black marble, surrounding the white marble chimney piece. And crimson and silver brocade striped curtains. The sofa and chairs are good – Edward says they came from Lancashire but can't remember how. They can be loose-covered in pale citron linen. And the carpet should be white. Fitted to the walls. And thick and fluffy.'

'I'm not sure that Edward . . .'

'Oh, and silver candlesticks with black candles on the chimney piece with a tall looking-glass behind them. It happens that I have some silver candlesticks somewhere. We used them in the Scottish Play. Now, let me go ahead.'

'The Chambers want to give us a wedding present,' said Filth three weeks later, standing outside the sitting-room door and wondering whether to remove his shoes. 'This white carpet. It's where we *eat*?'

'Oh, we'll eat in the kitchen now. It's beginning to be considered OK.'

'I'm sorry. I couldn't eat in a kitchen.'

'It's not like it used to be. It will be clean.'

'The Chambers', he said, in his bony stockinged feet, 'want to give us an armchair. I told them we have one coming from the East.'

'Dear love,' she said. 'We'll not see that again.'

Filth looked sad.

'What's wrong?'

'I remember your face when I bought it. Ecstasy.'

'Oh, I was being childish. Look, tell them we want a *black* chair from Woollands of Knightsbridge. I've seen it in the window. It has cut-out holes in it like Picasso. It sprawls about. It will add a revolutionary touch.'

When the chair arrived it still had the price tag attached. Twenty-two pounds!

'Crikey,' said Betty. 'Your Chambers must like you. We'd better give a party.'

'I never give parties,' said Filth. 'They know me.'

'They don't know me,' she said. 'Come on. I'll make a list. I've done coq-au-vin for dinner, all red gravy. It's in the kitchen.'

'Very well,' said Filth and, later, politely, 'Very good.'

'I wasn't sure about leaving the feet in.'

Filth's splendid face began slowly to crack into a smile. Regarding her, he began to laugh, a rare and rusty sound.

'Well, I was born in Tiensin,' she said.

'Do you know what you are, Elisabeth Feathers?'

'No?'

'You're happy. I am making you happy.'

'Yes. I am. You are. Come on. Eat up your feet.'

She thought about it as she cleared up the unconscionable amount of washing-up engendered by the coq-au-vin, as Edward sat in the Picasso chair, his papers for the next day fanning out all around him on the white carpet. Getting down to them on his knees for a moment, he got up covered in white fluff, but said nothing.

'You are happy,' said Delilah next morning over the garden wall as Betty hung out washing. 'What are those queer little tabs? Is it a variety of sanitary towel?'

'No, it's Edward's bands,' she said. 'Barristers' bands to tie round his neck in Court. They have to be starched every day. He used to have them sent out, which is fine in Hong Kong, but here – he says they are four pence each.'

'Aren't you going to get a job? Did you ever have one?'

'Yes. Foreign Service, once.'

'Oh. Clever, are you?'

'Yes. I am. Very. But I'm having a rest. I can't help it, Delilah, being clever. Oh, God!' The washing line came down in the flower bed.

'But when the baby comes?'

Betty, scrabbling and disentangling Edward's undergarments, froze.

'Well? I'm right, am I not? I can always tell. To an actress it is vital.'

Betty sat back on her heels, stared up at the flamboyant trees behind Delilah's head. Said nothing.

'Do I speak out of turn? Most humble apologies.'

'No, no, Delilah. Not at all.'

At length Betty said, 'Yes.'

'There's a doctor down the road. He's set up his brass plate, except that it is not brass but a piece of cardboard in the window. It is one of these new Indian doctors who are coming over. I believe they're very good, if you don't mind them touching you.'

Betty got up and went into the house and stood in thought. She stared at the white carpet.

'That will have to go,' she said.

She looked at the long windows open to the floor and the road below, and wondered if the balcony outside was strong. She smiled and addressed the black candles from the Scottish Play and said, 'I thought I couldn't be happier and I find that I am,' and alone she set off to the doctor.

And that day she walked and dreamed, smiling lovingly at every passer-by, crossing roads when lights were red, touching heads of children. At Buckingham Palace she stood gazing through the railings like a tourist. She crossed to the steps of the monument to Queen Victoria and looked up at the ugly, cross little face. Scores of children! she thought. And madly in love.

In St James's Park she leaned on the railing of the bridge and watched the ducks circling busily about and every duck became a celestial duck and the bridge was made of silver, and diamonds were scattered about on the muddy path. The willows swung and sighed over the water. She walked up Birdcage Walk and across Horse Guards Parade, shabby and colourless with wartime sandbags still here and there in sagging heaps. She walked past the door of Number 10 Downing Street that needed a coat of paint, and to the river that rolled deep and fast beside her and would do so long after she was dead. And the baby too.

She walked past the end of Northumberland Avenue, past Cleopatra's Needle, the flaking dying Savoy Hotel with its medieval-palace cellars. She walked up to the Strand, crossed over into Aldwych, up to the Temple and to Edward.

'Yes?' said the clerk, sharpish. 'What name please? Mr Feathers is in conference.'

'I'm Elisabeth Feathers. Betty Feathers. I've come to thank you for the chair.'

A clutch of girls behind massive typewriters all looked up at the same moment and a junior clerk, like Mr Polly in a stiff collar, dusted a chair and brought it for her.

'We can't disturb him,' said the clerk. 'I'm so sorry. But he won't be long. Congratulations on joining our Chambers!'

'Well, I'm not a barrister,' she said. 'Maybe I will be one day. I feel I could do anything. Oh, and we're giving a party.' As she spoke and they all sat observing her, she knew that she looked beautiful. Happiness makes you beautiful. I am happy and beautiful as an angel . . .

The door into the clerks' room opened and Edward came in and stopped, astounded.

Beside him, reaching not much above Edward's waist, stood Albert Ross.

'It's all right,' one of the typists was saying. 'Mrs Feathers? It's all right. You just fainted for a moment. Here. Water. All right? Sit up carefully.'

'Jet lag,' Edward was saying. 'We've been home for weeks, but we almost covered the globe on our honeymoon. Elisabeth, you've been working too hard at the bloody house.'

'Where is he?'

'Who?'

'Ross, Albert Ross. I thought I saw him standing beside you.'

'You did. He's gone. Don't worry, we'll both be seeing more of him soon. There's a big new Case in Hong Kong. Betty, sit quite still until they get us a taxi. I'll come back with you.'

'No. Don't fuss. I'm fine. I just couldn't stop walking. I walked all the way from home.'

'But it's miles! It must be four or five miles!'

'It was lovely. I just thought I'd call in.'

When Mr and Mrs Feathers had gone, Charles, the head clerk, went to the pub and the junior clerk for his sandwiches. The typists brought out their packed lunches and thermos flasks and cigarettes. One girl lay back in her chair. 'Pregnant,' she said. 'Well! Good old Filth.'

Chapter Seventeen

After the miscarriage of her child at four months, Elisabeth was to be in Hong Kong again with Edward and it was universally agreed that it would be excellent for her health. 'Look at the colour of you,' said Delilah. 'Milk-white, pinched and drawn, and staring eyes. Go back to your old friends and sit in the sun.'

'I like my new friends,' she said. 'I've never had friends I like better. I can stand on the doorstep in my dressing gown and watch the world go by. In Hong Kong they open the hotel door for me and I wear gloves and a hat to keep my English skin milk-white. Like my grandmother.'

'But you're not recovering. Not like us at your age. Gave thanks when it happened. Better than backstreets and penny royal.'

'Don't. Please.'

'I'm sorry, Elisabeth. Dexter and I had none, and we never felt the loss. We had each other. And work.'

Elisabeth drifted in her narrow garden. She didn't go out into the beautiful Regency crescents and squares behind

Mozart Electrics towards Knightsbridge and Hyde Park, where the war-torn houses were being returned to their natural composure. Old cottages built for nineteenth-century artisans, and mews houses and stables for grooms and horses round Chester Square, were going freehold for a song. 'We should buy one, I suppose,' said Edward. 'It might be useful.' But she refused to go to look.

The streets around Victoria were full of prams. Once she took a bus to Hyde Park ('for the air,' said Delilah) and there were wild rabbits in the bushes. The Peter Pan statue was being repaired in Kensington Gardens. Unchanged, the nannies in navy-blue uniform and pudding-basin hats were striding out behind baby carriages, each bearing a spotless baby. The war seemed to have made no difference. Some perambulators had crests painted on their flanks. When Elisabeth sat down on one particular park bench, two nannies approached her and one of them said, 'Excuse me, but this seat is only for *titled* families.' She walked the side streets after that but there was nothing that brought her comfort.

At last she said, 'Well, I'd better go to Edward.'

'You had. But I'll miss you,' said Delilah. 'Next time you're here you'll be laughing again. I promise. And we'll go to the music hall together and see *Late Joys*.'

Without saying goodbye to anyone she picked up a note Delilah had put through her letter box, looked across at the drawn curtains of the electrician who was getting up later and later now, and stepped into the taxi for the airport. She left no message for her new Jamaican cleaner, who had saved her life, because she could not face her. Even to think of her made her cry.

It had been the cleaner's morning.

Elisabeth had, from the start, given her her own key. Singing, the young woman had come tramping up the stairs, flung open Elisabeth's bedroom door, flung in the vacuum cleaner. Then stopped. Betty in bed. Eyes black pools. Sheets to chin.

'I'm losing the baby.'

'God a mercy! Where gone the doctor?'

'He came but he went. We've been expecting this. Things began to go wrong two weeks ago. He's coming back. He didn't think it'd happen yet. Well – I *suppose* he's coming back.'

'And sir? Does sir know?'

'I phoned.'

'When you phone, ma'am?'

'An hour ago. He's busy. He's finishing a set of papers.'

The woman plunged at the bedside telephone. Then she was yelling from the window on the street. Then she was calling from the back window on the gardens where Delilah was regarding her flowers. Then she was boiling water. Then she was propping open the street door with the bicycle so that the ambulance men could run straight through. She had found a chamber pot with roses painted round it and set it by the bed, soothing Betty and telling her it would soon be over now.

'It's coming in waves,' said Betty. 'It's like labour. Like they told us in the classes. Maybe I'm full-term? Maybe I'm just having a baby?'

'No, ma'am,' said the cleaner.

'Hold my hand,' said Betty.

'Give me this Chambers number. Right. Now then. Mr Feathers, this is your cleaner speakin'. You get you skinny arse home. Here. Now.'

A scuffle of people at the street door. The cleaner shouting down the stairs. A scream from the bed.

'Don't look, don't look,' Betty shouted to the cleaner. 'It's all over. It's in the . . .' and she screamed again. 'Get the dog out! The bloody dog.' It was Delilah's dog. A daily visitor. It sniffed the air. Then fled.

'It's the dog of the rat!' And she fainted. As she fainted she saw the little sliver of life slopped wet in the chamber pot. It had beautiful miniature hands.

Edward was too late to see. And too late to see her, for she had been taken off on a stretcher. Neighbours stood about the open door watching the arrival of the doctor, and the cleaner roaring at him. Edward had walked from the tube station, bringing with him his heavy briefcase to finish his work at home.

At the hospital they wouldn't let him see her.

Chapter Eighteen

A decade or so on, in their golden house in the row of judges' houses on the Peak, protected from the world which he was paid to judge and in which Elisabeth worked all the time with her charity work, certain friends would occasionally touch on the Feathers's childlessness. Betty, so fond of children – what a shame – etc. Betty had grown expert in her replies.

'Oh, I don't know. I don't think either of us was very child-minded. We knew nothing of children. We'd never had brothers or sisters ourselves. Poor Filth was a Raj orphan, you know. My parents died very young, too. We were ignorant.'

'You've had a wonderful marriage.'

'It's not over yet, thank you.'

(Ha, ha, ha.)

'You must have been a child yourself, Betty, when you married. So young.'

'Yes,' Elisabeth always said, 'I was.'

Hong Kong had embraced her again, wrapping her in its dazzle and warmth and noise: the smells of her childhood, the food of her childhood, the lack of false sentiment of her childhood. They took a furnished apartment on the Mid-levels and women friends came round for drinks and chat at lunchtime, and they went shopping with her in the blinding light of the big stores. She bought embroidered pillowcases and guest towels. She grew languid and lazy, and drifted away from Amy. Someone said that she should take up Bridge.

'Take her out of herself,' said a Scottish banker's wife to the wife of an English judge. 'Who hasn't had a mis?'

The other woman said that she had to drive up into the New Territories and Betty could come too.

'I'm looking for a rocking horse,' she said.

'A *rock*ing horse?'

'The grandchildren want one. We'll get it shipped home. They're twenty-five pounds in Harrods, and these are just as good. There's an old chap up there somewhere who makes them. They look a bit oriental but that's part of the fun. He sells them unpainted but then we could stipulate.'

'You mean stipple them? I don't think . . .'

'No, no – we could tell him what we want. A bay or a grey. That sort of thing. I'll ask the grandchildren in Richmond Gate what they'd like.'

'Is it tactful? Children's toys? If we're taking Betty?'

'Oh, come on. She's got to get over this and have another.'

So they set off into the New Territories in a smart little car, Betty smoking Piccadilly cigarettes. The city did not disappear so much as change and become a canyon between concrete cliffs of new housing for city workers. 'Further than this?' said the judge's wife looking at the map. 'I've never been as far as this. Oh yes, here's that little temple. In those trees. Shall we go in? Have a breather?'

It was midday and very hot. The courtyard of the temple was silent, its surrounding trees unmoving. There was no chatter of birds. On the temple steps a dead-looking dog lay like dried-out leather, one lip lifted as if in disdain. In the courtyard in front of the steps sat two old men at a table. They wore traditional black tunics and trousers, and one had a pigtail and a wisp of beard. They were playing chess under the trees and all was black and white except for the bold red lacquer of the soaring temple. Occasionally a grey leaf detached itself from the trees and fell about the chess players like pale rain.

'Well! You'd have thought they might have stood up,' said the banker's wife, 'as we went past. And I don't like the look of that dog. It's ill.'

'It's hot,' said Elisabeth. 'It's having its siesta like the whole of Hong Kong. Except us. And the chess players.'

'Well, don't go near it. A bite could kill. Oh, look here! This is monstrous!'

The temple steps were cracked and littered with papers and Coca-Cola cans, and the portico broken. The figures of the Buddha inside, arms raised, more than life-sized, were thick with dust. At a desk to one side, presumably selling things, a heavy girl lay sprawled asleep, head on arms. Her desk was thick with dust and dust seemed to emanate from the walls and ledges high above, resting on all the carvings like snow. The girl opened her eyes and made a half-hearted move to get up.

'Look here,' said the judge's wife. 'This won't do. What sort of impression does this make on the tourists?'

'Well, it's very Chinese, Audrey.'

'Not New Territories Chinese. It's all very well sending people to prison for graffiti on the new tower blocks where nobody goes except the workforce, but what about our own image here? This temple is in the guidebooks. Everyone comes.'

'There don't seem to have been many recently,' said Elisabeth.

'I'm not surprised,' said Audrey, and began to harangue the girl in execrable Cantonese. The girl drooped again, but said nothing.

'I think we should report this. I really do. Betty, have a word with Edward. I'll speak to Ronnie. We'll see they hear about it in Government House. It isn't fitting.'

'But it's their religion,' said Elisabeth. 'It's nothing to do with us. Perhaps dust doesn't matter to Buddhists.'

'Oh, but it's more than dust. It is slovenly.'

'And neglected,' said the banker's wife.

'It's theirs to neglect, I suppose,' said Elisabeth. 'If they wish to.'

'Hong Kong is still ours to administer,' said Audrey, and Elisabeth walked away, handing some dollars to the girl as she passed. The girl was pregnant.

Elisabeth went down the temple steps, stopping to stroke the dog, and her eyes were full of shame and tears as she stood in the glaring courtyard looking across at the chess players.

There was now a third man pondering the board. He was standing facing her, a blond European, dressed in khaki shirt and shorts, and when he looked up and across at her she saw that it was Veneering.

The querulous voices of the women floated out from the temple behind her and she walked forward across the courtyard towards Veneering's beckoning arm. He put his hand on her shoulder and said, 'Come with me. There are some seats lower down in the trees,' and they dropped down to a wooded track, passing the old men by. The old men did not stir.

There was a red-painted bench and they sat down and Veneering said, '*Whatever* are you doing out here?'

'I'm on the way to buy a rocking horse.'

They looked at each other for a minute or more and Veneering said, 'I heard that you have been ill.'

'Yes. The rocking horse is not for us. It's for one of the others. She's a granny.'

'Then she should have had the tact not to bring you.'

'She's one for soldiering on. Getting over things. Following the flag.'

'She sounds like my son Harry. He's a blimp.'

'How is he?'

Veneering smiled and said, 'Skiving off cricket. Says he has a limp. I've told him to go running. He'll get to Eton all right. Probably be a scholar.'

'Is he happy?'

'Oh, Harry's always happy.'

They fell silent and Elisabeth said, 'I didn't know you played chess.'

'It's just to keep up with Harry in the holidays.'

'Does Elsie . . .?'

He gave her a look.

'Give Harry my love,' she said. 'Is Elsie . . .?'

'It's Saturday. She's at the racecourse. Elisabeth, are you going to live here always with Edward?'

'Why?'

'Because if you are I'll have to go. I'm going to apply for a judgeship in Singapore. Hong Kong, the English Bar here – it's too small.'

She said nothing for a long time, and then they heard the women coming back down the steps of the temple and passing by them through the courtyard above.

'I want to go back to London now,' she said. 'I was so happy there after the – honeymoon.'

'And Edward?'

'Who knows where Edward is happy? He belongs to Asia. He was born here.'

'So they tell me. Betty, we can't go on. Both of us living here. You look so ill. So sad.'

'We may change.'

'Don't be ridiculous.'

'And I will never leave Edward. I must go. They're shrieking about, looking for me.'

'Give me your London number.'

'It's – we're – in the phone book. Don't ring me.'

She ran up the track and joined the other women in the car.

'Elisabeth! Where were you? You look exhausted.'

'Just wandering about.'

They roared off, erratic and talkative, towards the rocking-horse maker.

Chapter Nineteen

Elisabeth began to be elusive. She was not seen at anything. She sat staring out to the harbour below and said very little. 'You're not picking up,' Edward said one evening at the Repulse Bay Hotel where he'd taken her for dinner, the stars and moonlight magnificent. 'Betty, they're telling me you are ill.'

'Who?'

'Well, Willy and Dulcie, among others.'

'And are you worried?'

'I want you to see a doctor. Have a check-up. You were told to go back to a hospital in three months.'

'Was I?'

'You were. When they let you travel out here with me, you promised to see someone. They said the medicine here is very good. Well, we all know it is.'

'Oh, I'm just low.'

'I know. You are bound to be. It will take time. They told me you would need – er – cherishing.'

'And do you cherish me, Edward?'

'Well, I try. You frighten me these days, Elisabeth. I – well, I still can't' (the stutter threatened) 'quite get over my luck in having you. All the time.'

'Edward, how sweet!'

He looked at her. Watched for a sneer. Betty – sneering!

'Well, as a matter of fact, I'm scared of losing you,' he said.

One day, while he was at work, she rang up Amy who said, 'Come over.'

'Could you come here, Amy? It's not easy for me,' and Amy soon – though not as soon as she would have done once – arrived, and without a child in tow. They sat in Elisabeth's smart sitting room with drinks.

Amy said, 'You're drinking whisky.'

'Yes.'

'In the morning.'

'Yes. It's for the pain.'

'What pain?'

'Well, if you want to know, I'm bleeding. Most of the time.'

'You're *what*?! Great heavens, I'm taking you straight to the hospital. Now!'

'Oh, it's all right. I've always had trouble. For years after the Camp. There was nothing for years. Nobody menstruated. Then with me it began to go the other way. Embarrassing. Scarcely stopped. One of the pleasures of pregnancy was the relief from it.'

'Does Edward know?'

'Of course not. I don't think he's ever heard of menstruation. We sleep apart now, mostly.'

'But someone . . .'

'No. I'd probably have told Delilah. But you know, we *don't* talk about it, do we? Look at novels.'

'Be damned to novels, you're seeing a consultant.'

'Well, let's keep it from Edward.'

'Not on your nelly,' and she rang Edward to say she had made an appointment with a mainland-Chinese gynaecologist. Edinburgh-trained.

'Ah, Edinburgh-trained. That sounds very good, Edinburgh.' (The Scot speaking, though he had never been to Scotland.) 'I perhaps should go with her?' he said faintly.

'I don't want him,' said Elisabeth.

But the consultant thought otherwise and, after X-rays and examinations, telephoned Edward to tell him that he was to come with his wife to the hospital and bring with him a decent bottle of wine.

He told Edward that Elisabeth needed surgery. There was every sign of trouble. He believed that a complete hysterectomy might be necessary.

'But I'm not even thirty. I'm childless. *No!*'

'You've put your body – no, history has put your body – through hard times. You were half starved in the Internment Camp. And I believe you lost your parents?'

'Yes. It was all jolly rotten.' (Who is this speaking through my lips?) 'But I'm basically strong as a pit pony. Well, I *look* like a pit pony, don't I?'

Nobody laughed.

'Think about it. I can do the operation here, or I can send you to the best people in London. No, no – not Edinburgh. Too far from home. Your friends will be in London.'

'But Edward's in the middle of an Arbitration.'

'Think about it. But not for long. You should have it done *now*.'

Edward said, clearing his throat in his embarrassed and famous roar, 'Are you suggesting this might be cancer?'

'It's possible. I'll leave you to talk it over. Oh, dear – oh, hold on . . .'

Edward was gripping the edge of the doctor's desk and sliding to the floor.

'For heaven's sake!' Betty was holding him up in her arms and glaring at the doctor. 'Open the wine,' she said. 'Have you a corkscrew? Then you shouldn't have told us to bring it. Water, please.'

Amy was breastfeeding the newest child when Elisabeth arrived, the previous baby now crawling about and heaving itself up on supporting objects such as Mrs Baxter's difficult leg. Mrs Baxter was deep in a missal.

'Don't worry about her,' said Amy. 'She's not listening. Let me think.'

Elisabeth took the child on her lap. 'All I need to decide', she said, 'is whether to get it done here or in London.'

'Oh, London,' said Amy. 'No question. You'd be OK here but they're better with Chinese than European cancers.

There are different treatments. Look – go home at once, have it done, and let Edward fly back to see you when the thing adjourns. When is it? Within a month?'

'Yes. He's in a bit of a state. He doesn't speak.'

'Well, he'll be in a worse state if you go into hospital here. He'll have to be coming to see you every day from the other side of Kowloon. Maybe for two or three weeks. He'll concentrate better if you're far away.'

'D'you think so? Edward can always concentrate.'

'Yes, I do think so. And we'll all look after him.'

'You mean I just buy myself an air ticket and turn up in the Westminster Hospital all by myself?'

'Certainly. Why ever not? The bloke here will send them your medical records. What would you do if you weren't married? You'd get on with it by yourself.'

'Yes, indeed,' said Mrs Baxter, waking up. 'You must now be the Bride of Christ.'

'I always think that sounds blasphemous. And silly,' said Elisabeth.

'Well, Christ would say get on with it. Trust me,' said Amy. 'Think of the woman with the issue of blood for twelve years. Trust. You'll be rewarded.'

'Reward?' said Mrs Baxter. '*Is* there any reward? I'm beginning to doubt it.'

'Oh, Mrs Baxter, do shut up.'

'*I am lonely and bored,*' intoned Mrs Baxter. '*Reassure me, Good Lord.*'

'Mrs *Baxter*!'

'*And inform me about it. Is there any reward? I'm*

151

beginning to doubt it. Poor child, poor child,' she said. 'And scarcely left the altar.'

Elisabeth and Amy began to laugh. 'Wherever did you get that awful verse? This isn't a tragedy.'

'Not yet,' said Mrs Baxter.

It was from the moment of laughing that Elisabeth knew that she would recover. The knowledge that she would never have children lay deeper and she did not, presently, disturb it. Taking one thing at a time.

Chapter Twenty

The haemorrhaging that had been heavy but monthly had become fortnightly and then almost continuous, so that she travelled to London first class. She spent many of the fourteen hours' flight in the aircraft toilet to the distress of other passengers.

On landing, things let up for a while. The car that Edward had ordered was waiting for her and she was back in the embrace of the little house in Ebury Street within two hours of landing. Flowers had been sent by Edward and arranged on the black table by Delilah, with trailing leaves and swatches of blood-red roses falling like a ballerina's bouquet. There was food in the fridge, a bottle of wine, the bed made up. She rang the hospital, which expected her the day after tomorrow. 'You need to settle after the journey,' said the Almoner. 'And well done.'

The phone rang and it was Edward. The familiar lovely voice, the familiar understatements. Case going well. Missing her. Desmond and Tony taking him out to dinner.

Very civil of them. Amy had rung. He had forgotten to ask Betty if she had enough money.

'Yes. And I have forgotten to remind you that before long, I shall be thirty and come into my inheritance.'

He was not interested, and only said several times how much he felt he should be with her. But his voice did not convince.

The haemorrhaging came and went. She had begun to get used to it. She'd be glad to be rid of the whole beastly business. Blood, blood. Women and blood. The 'blood line'. Lady Macbeth. The phone rang again and it was Delilah next door. Should she come round? 'No. Sleep's what I want,' said Elisabeth, lying down on the bed.

But sleep is no part of jet lag, and blood and sleep are not good bedfellows. 'Oh, dear God,' she prayed in the beautiful plain bedroom with its lime-washed walls. 'Maybe I'd better ask them if I can go in now.' Tears came. 'Dear God – oh, it sounds like a letter – dear God, I can't suffer any more. No child will come out of this. I'm suffering more than if it was labour, and nothing at the end of it.'

The phone by the bedside rang and it was Veneering, in Hong Kong. 'You went Home then. Someone said so. Thank God. Look – Elisabeth, there is a very bad thing.'

'What? Edward? Not Edward, oh, God, no. No, we just spoke.'

'It's Harry. My son, Harry,' and the line fell silent. At last, when it revived, Veneering was in mid-sentence: '. . . operate tonight.'

'I missed that. The phone cracked up. What's happening?'

'Harry is very seriously ill. They've just had the X-ray of his leg. His femur. He's been limping . . .' The voice faded again.

'Yes? Terry?'

'The school had him to the local hospital and the X-rays show . . .' Emptiness again. Then 'show a hole in the femur the size of a hen's egg. The leg is on a thread. It's about to break. They want to operate tonight.'

'Tonight! Tonight? Where?'

'In south-west London. It's not far from you. It's a small hospital and there'll be a bed for you there. In Harry's room. It's the hospital this man likes – he's said to be the best surgeon in the world: but they always say that – it's where he likes to operate. I'll give you the number. The Housemaster's taking Harry in now and he'll stay until you come. He said he'd stay all the time, but was there somebody closer? I can't get there until tomorrow. I'm taking the first plane out. Will you go? Just be there during the operation?'

'Yes.'

'It's a miracle you're back in London. It was just the slightest hope. I had to ring. Yet I was sure you were in Hong Kong.'

'Tell me exactly where and when. I'll phone the school now.'

'He loves you, Betty.'

'And Elsie –?'

'Oh, she's coming over, too. The day after me.'

'I'll go at once. I'll try to be there ahead of him.'

'I love you, Betty.'

*

Ordering the taxi, scrabbling in her still-packed luggage for night things – medication, sanitary towels, sponge bag – she found that the haemorrhaging had stopped and she no longer felt ill. She thought of the woman in the Gospel whose issue of blood of twelve years had stopped as she touched Christ's garment so that he felt faint with the love she had drained from Him. Christ understood women. He romanticised nothing.

She arrived at the little hospital near Barnes Common ahead of Harry, and was told to wait in the room they were to share until he went down to theatre. Someone came in and asked her to go to see the surgeon who was standing in his consulting room examining X-rays, slotting them up on a wall against lights.

'Ah, come in and look at these, Mrs Veneering. Good afternoon.'

'No, I'm not a relation, just a close friend. I'm sorry. I'm a bit squeamish. I can't look. The father will soon be here. I'm so sorry.'

'Don't be squeamish. By tomorrow this X-ray will be far out of date.'

He flung down into a pedestal chair that began to revolve, this way and that. The music goes around and around, she thought. But no, it does not. The end is silence.

The surgeon stretched out his legs and rested his heels on a window ledge, the back of his head towards her. They both stared at the sun setting over Barnes Common.

'Mrs Veneering' – she thought: Oh, let it go – 'Mrs Veneering, we shan't know that this is cancer until I have seen it with my eyes, but when I do, I shall know at once. The cyst seems to have sharp sides to it. Cancer usually has a woolly edge. A turbulent look. I believe that there is just a hope that this is not cancer, and if not, I shall go on at once to fill the cavity with bone chips which we'll take from another part of Harry's body where we hope they will coagulate. The cavity is very big. The operation to fill it will take most of the night. The longer you wait the more hopeful you can be. If I come to see you quickly it will mean that it is bad news and we shall be stitching him up at once. Then you and I and Mr Veneering will talk together about the next step.'

'You mean there might be an amputation?'

'Oh, we won't talk about that now.'

'If it is cancer, how long will Harry live?'

'About eighteen months.'

'Does Mr Veneering know?'

'Yes. We spoke. But you will know the diagnosis before he does, as we are not able to reach him during the flight from Hong Kong. I want you, please, to stay here until he comes.'

'Well, yes. Of course.'

'You'll be in Harry's room and we'll see that you have supper. Don't drink any alcohol. It does not help.'

'Thank you.'

They shook hands and she said to him, 'How do you manage?' and his glance moved away from her and he began to straighten the pages on his desk.

'How do *you* manage?' he said. 'As a parent?'

*

When she got back to the room with the two beds there was Harry sitting waiting with his Housemaster from school. He was bright-eyed and making jokes, and when she came in he leaped to his feet and flung his arms round her neck.

'If it isn't Mrs Raincoat! Why ever are *you* here?'

'Your father sent me my orders.'

'He does have a cheek, my dad. I'm glad you're here, though. There's a great do on about my leg.'

'He's worried.'

'He's crazy. I'm fine. I mean, they're not going to cut it *off*. Goodbye, sir. Thank you for bringing me in. Sorry. I'm fine with Mrs Raincoat.'

'Your old nanny?'

'No,' said Elisabeth. 'But don't be embarrassed. It's been said before.'

'The school will be in touch all the time. You have the number?'

'I'll stay until Harry's father arrives.'

'Goodbye then, Veneering. Good luck. We'll be saying our prayers for you in Assembly.'

'It must be bad, then,' said Harry. 'That'll make them sit up. I'll be playing cricket again next season, sir. That'll disappoint them.'

'He got out pretty quick, didn't he? Was he glad to see you! Hey, Raincoat, what's it all about?'

'We'll know in the morning. Your father will be here. He's flying over now and I'll be standing by till he arrives.'

'Staying *here*? In the hospital? You must all be nuts.'

'Yes. I am, anyway. Now, be quiet and say your prayers. Here are a lot of people and a trolley, and they'll take you down to start things off any minute.'

'They're coming to take me away, tra-la,' said Harry. 'Goodbye. See you tomorrow, Raincoat.'

She left him being told to take off his shoes and she walked down the long green corridor towards the glass doors and the canteen and the trivial world. She took some food and coffee and sat down with it and looked at it. Then she got up and walked out of the hospital into the Upper Richmond Road where the people were tramping or driving or walking or biking about, and the grit was blowing in their faces. When she got back to the room it was empty and Harry's bed had only a sheet on it. Hers was turned down neatly for the night. The hospital was quiet and she felt light, without sensation or presence, and sat down on the basket chair that faced the door.

A nurse put her head round it, her face trying to disguise her pity with a smile that showed huge teeth. There was a row of the ugly new biro pens along her starched top pocket.

'There you are, Mrs Veneering. All right? Harry is in theatre now, and I expect you'd like a cup of tea.'

'No, thank you,' and she sat staring at the closed door asking God for the operation to be the long one. The long, exhausting, difficult, delicate one that would ensure that he would live for more than eighteen months.

'If I come to speak to you within the first hour,' he had said, 'that will be bad news.'

Dear God. Please do not let me hear him coming within

the first hour. Please let me wait all night long before I hear the sound of his feet. Tell me then how to bear the waiting. She listened, and in minutes heard the sound of his feet.

It was at that moment, very early morning in Kai Tak, that Amy woke up and began thinking about Elisabeth. She should now be safely in London, resting from the journey before going into the hospital on Wednesday.

Should she ring? All of three pounds? And it might upset Bets if she thought that Amy was nervous about her. Amy the strong? Or it might wake her up just as she'd got to sleep after a long flight.

But yes. Amy would ring.

In Ebury Street, opposite Mozart Electrics, the phone rang and rang and was not answered. Well, then, Amy would ring Edward before he left the Peninsular Hotel for the Arbitration and send love, and hope that all was well. Edward said: Yes, all was perfectly well. He had spoken to Betty just after she arrived home and she was going to be resting all day and tomorrow. Perhaps it would be best not to bother her, for she had sounded perfectly normal. Yes – a very good journey. Thank you, Amy!

Hmmh!

Then Isobel Ingoldby rang Amy in Kai Tak. Isobel was in Singapore, but she knew all about Elisabeth. She'd been trying to telephone her in London, but no reply. Had Amy any news?

'No. And it's odd she doesn't answer,' said Amy who had tried again. 'What about the neighbour? Shall I ring her?

She's called De-lilah Dexter, if you can believe. I could get her through International Enquiries.'

'I have her number,' said Isobel. 'If I don't ring you back it means that all's well.'

In half an hour Isobel rang Amy back. 'The Dexter saw her leaving the house just after she arrived home. She had an overnight bag with her and got into a taxi. She didn't say goodbye to anyone, and she left the front door wide open. No, she *isn't* at the Westminster Hospital. I rang it. She's expected there tomorrow. Look, I shouldn't worry. She'll be staying with a friend or something.'

'I might just ring Edward again. I could go round to the Arbitration,' said Amy. 'Or I could try to speak to the solicitor, the demon dwarf. He knows everything. Albert Ross. He's probably sitting in the Arbitration rooms.'

Isobel said, 'Well, be careful. He doesn't like Betty. He's bonded to Teddy with hoops of steel. He's frightening.'

'To hell with that,' said Amy, and left a message at the Arbitration for Albert Ross to ring her at lunchtime. Ross did not ring.

She rang again, and said that she was unhappy about her friend – her *school*friend – Mrs Feathers – who seemed to have disappeared from her London address. Ross did not call back.

At last she lost patience, phoned Nick to come home from work, left all the children except the baby with Mrs Baxter and turned up outside the conference room of the hotel where the Arbitration was being held and marched in.

The room was empty.

She sat down for a minute in the cigarette smoke. There were ashtrays and a few scattered pens, and a disquiet in the air. Then she flung off again to the hotel's reception desk.

'They have adjourned,' said the concierge. 'The Counsel for the contractors has had to fly suddenly to London. Illness. A child.'

'Good heavens! Mr Feathers? But I spoke to him today.'

'No, Mr Feathers is for the architects. This is Mr Veneering. Would you like to speak to Mr Feathers's instructing solicitor? He could tell you more. He is somewhere about.'

'No. Thank you. It's rather confusing. This is all to do with *Mrs* Feathers. It's nothing to do with Mr Ross.'

'Ah, but it is,' said Ross behind them, and she turned and saw that he was seated in the foyer, his legs stuck out before him showing the soles of his tiny feet, his great head a sort of centrepiece to the mound of orchids and potted palms arranged on the marble floor. His hat lay beside him.

Ross did not look up from his playing cards as she walked across to him, the baby on her hip, and, still without looking at her, he said, 'Mrs Feathers has gone off with Mr Veneering. Mr Feathers does not know. I know, but no one else knows. I shall see that the matter is resolved. Mr Feathers will *never* know, and if you or Miss Isobel Ingoldby ever let him know, I will break you. Is that clear? I will break you both.'

Chapter Twenty-one

'If I come to speak to you within the first hour of the operation', the surgeon had said, 'that will be to bring bad news. I have to make this clear. You do understand?'

'Yes.'

It was hardly half an hour since they had brought her tea and told her that the operation had begun when she heard the swing doors slam-bang at the end of the corridor and feet running.

Of course the feet need not be his. Harry could not be the only patient in this silent little hospital. The feet were running. It could be anyone. But the feet stopped outside her door. And at the same moment she realised that the feet had been *running*. Nobody runs to break bad news. The feet had been *running*!

She stood up and a man opened the door clumsily, pushing it with his shoulder. He had a turban of dark green cloth round his head and a green apron tied about with tapes. He was holding up his hands and arms at right-angles from the elbow as if he were a priest at votive

offering. Or maybe a janitor. There was a smell of disin-
fectant.

The eyes, however, were the surgeon's eyes, very bright.
He said, 'Mrs Veneering, all is well. All will be perfectly
well,' and was gone.

All she could think was: now he will have to take all that off
and scrub up again before he can go back to do the chips of
bone. And she sat down again and looked at the closed
door.

She sat on and on until someone suggested she changed
into night things and went to bed. 'I shan't sleep,' she said,
but slept almost at once.

When she woke she was in familiar trouble, gathering
her towel and sponge bag and clothes, finding a bathroom.
Returning, two solid young nurses were looking down at her
sheets with amazement. In shame – she could not say one
word to them – she went along to the duty nurse outside,
and the duty nurse smiled at her.

It was the toothy nurse. 'I can see into theatre from my
little room,' she said. 'The lights were on all night. It must
have been *nine hours*! I thought, "Oh, that poor boy, he's
still in there. But he's alive. They'll get him back."'

'It's not, after all, cancer, nurse. Did you know?'

'Oh, we all know. Word went round. All round the hospital. We've all been thinking of you.'

'Thank you.'

'Mr Veneering's just arrived. They're telling him the good
news downstairs.'

'Then', said Elisabeth, 'I'll go. I'm not Harry's mother, nurse, but I know his father very well. They'll both be all right now. They won't need me.'

At the entrance to the hospital she asked the desk to get her a taxi and kindly ring the Westminster Hospital – she gave them the correct extension – to say that she was coming in this morning, at once.

Chapter Twenty-two

Her hysterectomy, the nurses told her the next day, had been 'very necessary'.

'There were precancerous cells,' said the surgeon. 'They were in one ovary and the womb is gone too, but we have left you with the other ovary so that you won't suffer a premature menopause.'

'Thank you.'

'We're really delighted that you came to us so quickly. And just in time. You are young and strong, Mrs Feathers. Is your husband about the hospital today?'

'He's about his work on the other side of the world.'

'Brave girl. Brave girl.'

(Oh, shut up, she thought. Meet Amy.)

'And he will soon be coming back? You are going to need a lot of care. Have you any children who could help?'

'No. I am not yet thirty.'

'Oh, yes. Yes, of course. I'm sorry.'

'Not as sorry as I am.'

*

Yesterday when they returned her to the ward after the operation she had partly woken and found that she had changed sex and century. She was a man, a soldier being tipped into some sort of mass grave. She smelled the wet earth of France. When she woke much later there was sunlight all round her body, which was neatly arranged under a thick white sheet. Bouquets and clumps of flowers were all around her. I am on my catafalque. And I have woken up. How embarrassing for them. I will sit up very slowly in the middle of the service as they sing me out. Someone pushed her down against a pillow and, when she woke next, Filth was sitting by the bed, reading *The Times*. He glanced across, saw her open eyes and smiled, stretching to her hands and kissing her fingers and wrists.

'You came,' she said.

And he said, 'Of course. I'm going back on Monday. Short adjournment.'

'You'll kill yourself. Jet lag –' and dropped asleep.

When she next woke he was asleep in the chair, and she watched his peaceful face.

'He is open as the day.'

'What?' he said. 'What?'

'You are as open as the day.'

'Why should a day be open? I've often wondered. Some days are sealed off, thanks be. I don't want to open up the day of your operation again.'

'I thought of you. Now and then.'

'Needless to say, the other side was to have been Veneering, but he bunked off back to London. Left his junior, a useless fellow, and I ran him into the earth in double-quick time. I got here for breakfast. Saw two moons rise.'

'Shall you see two more rise, going back?'

'I didn't come here to look at moons.' He rested his head against their clasped hands on the bed sheet.

She said, 'I'm sorry, Edward. No children now,' and slept.

She woke again and he said, 'D'you know, I never really wanted any children. Only you.'

When she woke next he had gone, and when she left the hospital two full weeks later it was with Isobel Ingoldby.

She had found Isobel standing at the foot of the bed, as tall as a camel and eating a pear.

'Home,' she said. 'I'm taking you.'

'Oh, Lizzie. Lizzie-Izz.'

'Wrap yourself up. It's turning towards autumn. Get this on over your sweater.' It was a brown and gold pashmina, warm and light and smelling of spices.

The nurses were kind, full of congratulations about how well she had done. They settled her into a taxi and into the world again.

'But we're not going towards Pimlico! Lizzie, we've missed the roundabout.'

'Yes.'

'Izz, why aren't we going to Ebury Street?'

'Because we're going to the Temple.'

'That's wrong. That's Eddie's Chambers. It's *wrong*. We have this flimsy lovely house in Ebury Street.'

'Talk later,' said Isobel. 'I just do what I'm told. Here's the Embankment, and we drive under the gateway and – my goodness! Teddy's certainly made his mark. The Inner Temple! Here's your new apartment. Gor-blimey, first floor, looking at the river.'

'But where's all our . . . Where's my *house*? Our white carpet? Wedding presents? What's Eddie been up to? The black chair?'

'I've no idea. There seems to be plenty still to unpack. There's a huge *red* chair, none too clean. *Superb* rooms! However did he get them? Rooms in the Temple are like gold. Oh, well, I suppose he is made of gold now. Mr Midas.'

Elisabeth walked to the window and looked across the river at the rising post-war blocks of cement.

She said, 'What's happened to them? They'll have got bread and milk in for me, and ordered the papers. They'll worry.'

'Hush. Too soon.'

'Tell me.'

'No. Well, oh, all right. Ebury Street is being pulled down. The hospital knew but didn't want to tell you. You said it was fragile. All the bombing . . .'

'Pulled down! No! Not in three weeks.'

'No. Not yet. But they've started demolition at the Victoria end. They said – your pals – "Don't let her come back." They've mostly been rehoused already.'

'What about Mozart Electrics? Across the road?'

'Someone told me – I went round there – that he's gone into a home. Very crippled.'

'And Delilah? And the butler? And the greengrocer?'

'The greengrocer's gone to Lowestoft. I found the building firm. Teddy had organised the furniture to come here to the Temple and they gave me a key to have a look around. I collected your post off the floor.'

Elisabeth stood watching the river for some silent minutes and said, 'Well, he's taken everything from me now.'

'Oh,' said Isobel. '*No*! Poor Teddy! And working like hell.'

'He could have told me.'

'He was told not to upset you. The Chambers know. They'll be coming. He arranged everything, except me. He doesn't know we know each other – remember?'

'Yes. But I forget why.'

'Don't think too hard. Listen, you're going to have help here – shopping and ironing and so on.'

'You are *crowing*!'

'Why? *Crowing*? Me?'

'Because I shouldn't have married him. You said so.'

'God's truth!' shouted Isobel. 'I traipse round builders, I look up neighbours, I get your post, I fetch you home . . .'

Elisabeth turned back to the river and said, 'Had they started the demolition?'

'Yes. The bank on the corner has closed and the little paper shop, and there's scaffolding up. At the back in those gardens . . .'

'Yes?'

'They were chopping down the trees. Listen, get Teddy home and stop crying. You're menopausal.'

'I can't. I'm not. I'm rational and sad,' she said.

'Then go off with bloody Veneering! I can't do more,' and Isobel slammed away.

Elisabeth walked to another window in the new lodgings, to try to see Lizzie cross the Temple yard towards the alley to the Strand and the Law Courts. It was very quiet in the new apartment that was presumably now her home. She saw that there were flowers in cellophane with cards pinned to them, a pile of letters on a desk. She looked in the one small bedroom with two single beds, fitted end to end. A midget kitchen and a bathroom made for giants, with a bath on feet. And silence. Silence from the corridor outside and the scene below, and from the uncaring river.

She thought: I'm on an island in an empty sea. I'm cast away. Her legs felt shaky and she sat down, trying to remember that being alone was what most of the world found usual. She thought that in childhood she'd been in crowded Tiensin, a crowd of Chinese servants day and night. In the Shanghai Camp, people and people, a slot in a seething tent; my hand always held by my mother, or riding on my father's back. The crowded ship to England, the crowded London school, the crowds of students at her all-women Oxford college, the return to Hong Kong and the infrastructure of Edward's world. Now this solitude. Double-glazed silence. I suppose I must just wait. It's the anaesthetic still inside me. I have memory, so I must still be here. I have nobody, but I have memory. There was a knock on the door.

But the door of the apartment seemed a mile away and she could not move. She stared at the door and willed it to open of its own accord and after a moment it did, and Albert Ross walked in.

'No! Get out! Go away!'

He took off the broad brown hat and sat down on the red chair and looked at her from across the room.

'Go away. I hate you.'

He twirled his shoes, regarded them and, without looking at her, said, 'I've come to apologise. I dealt you the Five of Clubs. It was a mistake. I seldom make a mistake, and I have never apologised for anything before, being of a proud nature.'

She watched him.

'The Five of Clubs means "a prudent marriage not for love".'

She watched him.

'I am very much attached to your husband. I saw only your faithlessness. It affected the pack. I was wrong.'

'You were always wrong. You stole his watch once.'

He became purple in the face with rage and said, '*Never*! He gave it to me when I had nothing. It was all he possessed. He trusted me. It was to save my life.'

'You are cruel!'

'Here is a telephone number you must ring. It will be to your advantage.'

'I don't need your help.'

He sighed and put out a hand to his hat and she thought, He may have a knife. He could kill me. He is a troll from a stinking pit.

But he brought out of the hat only the pack of cards, looked at it, then put it away.

'This is a transition time for you. You still don't see your way. This telephone number is from someone who cares about you. Her name is Dexter,' and he put a visiting card on the table and was gone.

A dream, she thought.

She did not move, but slept for a minute or perhaps an hour, then crossed to the table where there was no visiting card. She searched everywhere, under the table, even along the passage outside the door. Nothing.

Then the telephone rang and a voice said, 'Might I have the honour of addressing Mrs Edward *Feathers*?'

'Delilah!'

'Aha,' said the familiar phantom voice. 'Seek and ye shall find! I am speaking from the West Country. From Dorsetshire. England.'

'Dorset?'

'You will remember that we have our country estate in Dorset? Well, it is, by some, designated "country cottage". Now that we have been cast out of our London home, we have taken refuge in it.'

'But where exactly, Delilah?'

'Well, we are not *exactly* on the estate, but some fifty miles away in the fine city of Bath where mercifully Dexter has been granted God's gift of *The Admirable Crichton*.'

'Who –?'

'The *comedy* of that name written in honour of the

immortal figure of the English butler. Second only to the incomparable *Jeeves*. Five performances a week plus matinées, good cheap theatrical lodgings thrown in. Alas, however, he is in at the final curtain every night and grows a little wearier each day.'

'Oh, Delilah!'

'But we find ourselves affluent, well-housed, awaiting the compensation for our London home. Our country property is deserted. We hear that you are recovering from surgery and our little empty dacha in the woods awaits you, if you would like to stay in it. For ever, if you like.'

'Like to!'

'It is yours to use as long as you like. I am in touch with dear Eddie's clerk. He will make all the arrangements. Why do you weep?'

'With joy and disbelief. Oh, Delilah, it's like a musical!'

'There is, I fear, no music at our dacha,' she said, 'except the music of the rooks and the morning chorus of a myriad other species of feathered creature; the pizzicato of the rain and the crashing tympani and singing strings of the west wind. There's no electricity, dear, no running water and no abominable telephone.'

'Oh, it's *not* abominable! How else could we be talking?'

'Milk and bread are delivered daily to the lane – a little climb up from the back of the house. Also the daily papers. You can give them lists of groceries and you will pay in the basket provided before you go home. No one will disturb you. Dexter has a splendid theatrical library, if a trifle damp, and there is the evening softness of lamplight.'

'Delilah – I'm a bit potty at the moment. I've had surgery and I'm still full of anaesthetic. I've just had a hallucination. Is this another?'

'Hallucination, dear? No. Hallucination demands vision. Nor am I an aural manifestation. The return fare from Waterloo to Tisbury Junction is modest, and you will be met. Contact Eddie's clerk. Bring a wrap for the early mornings so that you can walk in the dew. And an insect repellent. You will be quite alone.'

'Are we going to meet there, Delilah – dear, beloved Delilah? I'm so bloody lonely.'

'Very good for you, dear. And I hardly think we'll meet. My duties to Dexter are very onerous. He sends his love. We shall possibly meet again one day, of course. These things may happen. I don't suppose' – her voice trailed away to nothing, then came back like a thread on a lute string – 'you've heard anything about the gardens? They haven't cut them down, have they? My London forest trees?'

She said, 'No, no. I'm sure not,' and the line clicked shut.

But the phone number? She couldn't call Delilah back. She must telephone Chambers. She must think of timetables on the Southern Railway. She must make lists of supplies. She must phone Edward. She must think of supper.

In the fridge she found milk and food, and on the table yet another bouquet of flowers from Edward and a note from the Inn with the times of Sunday services at the Temple church. Then the phone began to ring again and again, friends from near and far. The world grew smaller and smaller and so crammed with kind enquiries that she left the receiver off. Kind and rowdy, the city surged up to her from the river and the Embankment and the Strand, rich and glorious. Tomorrow she would be coping with rooks.

Then she saw, in the mail on the desk, a packet from Hong Kong lying beside the cards and she took it across the room and slowly and carefully opened it. Inside was a short double string of pearls with a diamond clasp and a note saying, *He is better. He will live. Return these at your peril. For ever V. PS: Where did you go?*

Chapter Twenty-three

It was a train ride of pure celebration. A train ride like childhood's. Edward's Chambers saw her on to the platform and right into the reserved seat for Tisbury Junction. The clerks gave her chocolates and told her that there would be a taxi waiting. At Tisbury she climbed out upon the single-track platform and sat on a seat in the sun and, like an old film, a man came along and said in a country voice, 'Taxi, ma'am? Let me take your case.'

He drove along the lanes and she saw a tree above a hedge like a hen on a nest, then a long stone wall, and in a gap in the wall she looked down upon a dell and a massive stone chimney pot attached to something unseen. The driver and the bag went ahead down the slope until they were on a level with the chimney pot and looking at an almost vertical track below and a thatched roof.

'I'll never get the case down there. This must be the back. There must be a front way somewhere.'

'What shall we do?'

'I'll have a try.'

He trundled and slithered, Elisabeth following, and they arrived at a paved yard and a back door. She paid him.

'You OK here, miss?'

'Yes,' she said, liking the 'miss'. 'Thank you,' and leaving the luggage in the grass, she went looking for the front door where she had been told there would be a key under a mat. She could find neither door nor key, and the silent valley beyond watched. In an outhouse which was an earth closet there was a huge black iron key and she thought she would try it in the back door, and set off further round the gentle, sleeping house and came to a front door with a Yale key in it, waiting to be turned. Inside were dark rooms and the smell of damp books. She saw furniture under dust sheets, a paraffin lamp with a cloudy globe, a box of matches alongside and a fresh loaf on the table.

It was not yet dusk and so, after standing a kettle on a black stove that seemed to be warm, she walked outside again into the garden.

It was a glade cut out from woodland. The stretch of grass that led to more faraway trees was not so much lawn as meadow, where vanished trees were waiting somewhere to reclaim their home. She felt the stirring of life under the grass and saw spirals of bindweed standing several feet high seeking some remembered support. They swayed as if they were growing under water. There was nothing more, only the dwindling path, the dwindling light, the pearly quiet sky.

She returned to the house, removed the kettle, found a staircase behind a cupboard door, reached a bedroom with wooden walls and smelling of cedar trees. She opened the window and looked at the glimmer of the evening and without even a drink of water, without locking the house or turning a key or taking off her coat, she lay down on the patchwork quilt and listened to the end of the day. Soon all the small sounds stopped, and she slept.

It was an eerie dawn, blowy and cloudy, and she had no idea where she was. When she remembered, she listened for the rooks but they were silent. She was afraid for a while that yesterday's journey belonged to someone else. Then, rolling from the bed, walking to the window, she saw that this was a strange place but in some way she knew it. The window looked at a wall of vegetation so close to the glass that she could stretch and touch if she opened it. She saw the roof of a shed that must be the earth closet. Yet she had remembered golden space.

And then she remembered that she had chosen the tiny back bedroom to sleep in. The other room with its mighty feather bed had seemed too intimately a part of the Dexters' lives to disturb. She went downstairs, dragged the black kettle across the wood-burning stove until it was over the hotplate – still hot. More wood was needed and when she looked, there it was. She found a tin teapot and a tea caddy that said it was a present from Blackpool. A jug of milk stood in a bowl of water on the pantry floor. Across the top, it had a muslin cloth weighted down with little coloured beads. The pantry stones were cool under her bare feet.

She carried her tea with her towards a door – the cottage

was shadowy – which she pushed open to reveal the stretch of meadow-lawn cleared from the forest. The trees around were wildly tossing and the grass was wet with dew. A fox stood still in the middle of the space, staring at her with black eyes, interested in an alteration of the scene. A dead bird hung down heavy and soft on either side of the fox's mouth. It turned tiptoe on its black feet and was gone. Then the wind dropped and lemon-coloured light soaked over the garden and the river spread wide to the horizon where above the far trees a triangle of hilltop was crowned with a knot of trees like a garland.

It was warmer now. She sat outside on the shabby wooden balcony and drank the tea. She thought of her new London home that commanded a view of a thousand nameless lives. Here she was alone of her kind. She felt perfectly happy, no more lonely than the fox, or the rabbits she began to see in the bracken, or the strutting pheasant which appeared now at her feet. No telephone would ring, no car stop on the road above, she would hear no human voice.

Amy, in her Kai Tak slum, would say, 'Betty, this will not do. You need a cause.' Elisabeth thought of the hollow-cheeked crowds in the stinking streets. The old man who sat with no legs, his crutches splayed across his patch of the street, breaking open crustaceans, chanting the prices, cracking the shells. Urine in the pools. 'We must forget *ourselves*, Bets. Our Englishness.' Amy had not been in the Camps.

She sat on, looking towards the topknot garland of the next-door village and saw to one side of her, higher up than the Dexter trees, a flicker. There must be a building up there, and her heart plunged. No – too dense. An illusion. She looked back down her vista of meadow, and two children were walking hand in hand. They paid her no attention and slipped back into the tall grass. Later, a young man crossed from one side of the garden to the other but further away. He was lean, unkempt, dark-skinned, alert and self-contained. Some sort of gypsy. He was swinging something like an axe and did not look towards the house. She heard the distant sound of the car bringing her groceries on the road above. The rooks began their civic racket. I must decide what to do with the day, she thought. But not yet.

On the balcony was a long wooden chair with a footrest and padded cushions, and she thought: That will be damp, but lay down and found it warm and sweet-smelling, and she fell asleep again.

All week she stayed alone in the house and garden, collecting groceries from the top of the steep slope, leaving money and details of supplies for the next day. A can of soup, a piece of cheese, three apples. She worried at first about water. Someone had left out two jugs on the slab in the pantry, otherwise there was only a stream. She washed in the stream, boiled some of it, eventually drank it unboiled, catching it in a tin mug as it rushed by. She liked the earth closet. Seated there, the door wide to the view, she commanded territory crossed by Roman cohorts on the march to Salisbury.

On the third day she began to notice things to do in the garden and spent a morning getting out weeds, shouldering them in armloads to what seemed to be a compost heap. She amazed herself. She did not know where her knowledge came from. She marvelled at the rich soil – remembering the scratching in the earth by the skin-and-bone labourers in the lampshade hats of her Chinese childhood. She imagined a continuing supply of vegetables, and, along an old red wall, a sea of European tulips. Then she remembered that this was Delilah's garden.

In the evenings, after a first attempt when black flakes flew to the ceiling and the wick roared like a petrol fire, she mastered the oil lamp and sat reading the books about old theatre productions and biographies of great actors. Sometimes, prising a book out of the damp shelves, she let loose a sheaf of theatre programmes. Some were signed flamboyantly with forgotten names, some smelled of long-dead violets. Once or twice a pressed flower fell out – a gardenia (gone brown) or a rose – and crumpled before her eyes when she tried to pick it up. Some of the books were inscribed *To my darling Delilah, the ultimate Desdemona* or *To my own Mark Antony from his adoring wife* and the date of over half a century ago.

Love, thought Elisabeth. Adoration. Was it all just theatre?

Chapter Twenty-four

One day she woke up and forced herself to think: when am I going home?

In fact she knew the date. Somewhere it was written down, perhaps on her return railway ticket. A taxi was to pick her up that morning, to put her back on the London train. She remembered that.

But when was it? She had no way of knowing the date: no radio, no daily paper. Letters had come for her but she had not opened them and they would not have helped. She would ask the village shop to put tomorrow's newspaper in with her baked beans. They would not keep the *Telegraph* or *The Times* or the *Manchester Guardian*. Perhaps they only had the weekly local paper. She thought she'd try for the *Daily Express*. When she collected it, she found that she had only one day left. This day. The taxi would be here to take her towards London before nine o'clock tomorrow morning.

She could hardly bear it.

Suppose she ran from the house tomorrow and hid in the

woods? She could creep back again in the evening. Or on another evening? She could sleep in the woods.

But then, word would go round. The village shop (wherever it was) would come making enquiries. Friends in London – Chambers – even Edward in Hong Kong.

I'm still trapped, she thought. I'll have to go.

She cleared the kitchen of the glorious squalor she had made in it. She dusted. She trimmed the lamp, thinking that there were very few people left in the world who could trim a lamp (and where had she learned? And when?). Fitting back its beautiful globe, she smashed it to pieces and was horrified. The lamplight had been the wonder of her evenings and the carrying up of the heavy lamp, one hand shading the light, to bed at night. Oh, Delilah! Oh, if there were a telephone . . .

Well, no. Thank God. And I don't know the number. I shall leave you, Delilah, a huge sum of money to replace the lamp. I shall scout the London markets for a new one.

She scrubbed the whole house clean. That evening, she walked down the garden and looked at the red wall in the fading light. The rooks grumbled their way to bed.

In the morning she gathered her things together around the door and ate some bread. There was a fumbling shadow outside the window, and she saw the gypsy person ambling about outside. He was trying to look in.

'Yes?' she called, not opening the door. 'Yes?' He was trailing the thing like an axe. 'Who are you?'

He mouthed words at her. She thought: the poor thing's simple. But the axe made her hesitate. He was speaking of a key. He needed a key. The taxi would be coming.

'But the *axe*,' she said.

'It's for the w-w-w-wood. Firewood.'

She brought him in. 'I'm so sorry. I was afraid of you.'

Among the things she had been leaving for the Dexters were two bottles of village-shop wine and she handed them now to the gypsy. He looked bewildered so she gave him some money. He took the key and the money and went ahead of her with her case and, when she was through the front door, he locked it behind her and put the key in his pocket. He went ahead, up the steep bank through the slit in the wall, not helping her, and when she had climbed the perilous slope there was her suitcase beside the road, and he was gone.

She sat down then on a stone on the roadside, her back to the wall. It was not yet a quarter past eight. It was beginning to be cloudy. Cloudy and wettish. England in October, although it was only September. Nobody passed by.

I had to be here for the taxi, she thought, before nine. I hadn't thought of rain. It's only eight-twenty.

Out of her bag she dragged the brown and gold pashmina and wrapped it round her. When the rain began she rearranged the coloured silk to cover her head. Bright against the dark bushes she sat on in the rain and when the village shop van passed she waved, but she had paid her bill yesterday and the car went by.

Nobody came. The rain became heavier. It was after half past eight now and the wind blew the rain in surges and began to sound angry and bitter. The rain lashed back.

Elisabeth looked up the road and down it, and wondered

how far it was to the village. Below her, the cottage was all securely locked up. Maybe she should stumble down the slippery path again and shelter in the earth closet.

No. Ridiculous. The taxi was taking her to catch a particular train. At Waterloo Station a cab had been ordered by Edward's Chambers to take her back to the flat in the Temple. All arranged. Foolproof.

But no taxi.

I'll go and see if there *is* a house up there, she thought, and shuddered. She was frightened of houses in woods.

No. She would walk into Salisbury, carrying her suitcase. Her scar still hurt and still bled a little but she didn't care. She tightened the silk cloth about her, picked up her suitcase and heard the sound of an approaching car. Thank God! Oh, thank God!

She stood holding the suitcase as the car spun into sight and it was not a taxi, but an ordinary private car going by. It was travelling very fast and splashed past her and down the hill, and vanished round the bend in the road and was gone.

So much, she thought, for answers to prayer.

She gripped the handle of her suitcase tighter, turned to face what she hoped would be Salisbury, soaked now to the skin, and heard the same car roaring back again up the hill, so fast that she had to jump into the side of the hedge.

The car stopped, the driver's door flew open and Edward stood in the middle of the road.

Wet to the skin, enclosed in his long arms, Elisabeth began to cry and Edward to set up the curious roaring noises that had overtaken him since his stammering childhood but now only when he was on the point of tears.

She said, 'Oh, Eddie! Oh, Filth!' her wet face against his clean, warm shirt.

She thought: I love him.

He said, 'I thought you'd left me!'

PART FOUR:
Life After Death

Chapter Twenty-five

Scene: Hong Kong.

Crackle and swish of limousine bringing the Judge home from court at exactly the appointed hour (insert clock: seven p.m.).

Interior. Elisabeth waiting for him in living room of Judges' Lodgings, a row of mansions behind a wall and steel gates, guarded. She has an open library book face down upon her knee. Outside, Edward Feathers's driver rings the front-door bell.

Elisabeth counts silently. A full minute. Longer. Two minutes.

Slip-slop feet of Lily Woo from kitchen across polished hall.

Lily Woo: Good evening, sir.

Slip-slop she goes back.

Edward takes off shoes in hall. Clonk, then clonk. Puts on house shoes left him there by Lily. We hear him go to wash in cloakroom. He opens living-room door and sees Elisabeth as ever waiting. (Pretty dress, neat hair, gold chains, perfect fingernails. She is changed.)

Edward (Filth): Gin? All well?

Elisabeth: Yes, please. And no. Not all well. Today I've had a revelation. I am now officially old.

Filth: Ice? Old?

Elisabeth: Yes, and yes. Today I heard myself telling someone on the Children's Aid committee that we'd been living in Hong Kong for over twenty years and that it seems no more than about six; and where did all the years go? Saying that, I'm old.

Filth: God knows where they've gone. Into the mist.

Bell rings outside in hall. Tinkle, tinkle. It is a small brass honeymoon bell from India. Slip-slop of girl's feet again as she returns to kitchen. Filth looks into his gin and vermouth and gulps it down.

Elisabeth: You're drinking too fast. Again.

Filth: I need it. Various things. What's this, being old?

Elisabeth: I feel it. Suddenly. I'm melancholy at things changing. So, I'm old.

Filth: They need to change. It's a place of changes. Annexing Hong Kong set the scene for change at the start. It will never settle down. Never be contented. But what did we bring but good? Work. Medicine. The English language. The Christian faith. And the Law. With all its shortcomings, they don't want to change the Law.

Goes over to the drinks tray.

Elisabeth: That was the dressing bell. Dinner in twenty minutes.
Filth: Or three-quarters of an hour. She's sloppy.
Elisabeth: Yes. Go on. Go up. Have a shower and change your shirt. You can have a whisky after dinner.

Scene: Dining Room.
A quiet dinner. The silver and glasses are reflected in the rosewood dining table. Lamb chops, peas, new potatoes. (Lily Woo has learned to cook them very well and sometimes it is a pleasant change from chopsticks.) English vicarage tonight.

Filth: It would be good to finish off with cheese now.
Elisabeth: It would be astonishing to finish off with cheese. There's not a speck of it in the Colony. Your mind is going!

After dinner, Filth stares at tomorrow's Court papers. He goes to bed early, without the whisky. In the middle of the night Elisabeth wakes to find him in her bed, his head on her breast. She takes him in her arms.

Filth:	I condemned a man to death today.
Elisabeth:	I know. I saw the evening paper. Was he guilty?
Filth:	Guilty as hell. It was a *crime passionnel*.
Elisabeth:	Then he is probably glad to die.

They lie awake for a long time. The hanging will be at eight o'clock. Elisabeth has set the bedside clock half an hour fast, and seen that Lily Woo has done the same to the grandfather striking clock downstairs. They lie awake together.

Filth:	Capital punishment must go.
Elisabeth:	They'll take years.
Filth:	They'll have their own Judiciary by then. Someone spat at the car today when I left Court. They are changing. Lily Woo took five minutes to answer the bell tonight.
Elisabeth:	No, only two. But I know what you mean. Respect is fading. Well, I don't know if it was ever there. In the jewellers', the girls hardly bother to lift their heads when I go in. They just go on threading the jade. They used to get me the best stones. They still get them for Nellie Wee.

Filth:	Oh, well. She's famous.
Elisabeth:	Well, I'm quite famous. I do my best. I try to be like Amy used to be. I *have* got the OBE. And half my girlfriends are Chinese.
Filth:	I used to say that when you were sifting through the jade in the market your eyes changed to slits and you became an Oriental.
Elisabeth:	Slits, with English eyelashes. Filth, we do need to live out here, don't we? We're lifetime expats. Aren't we?

Filth (after a long, long pause): I don't know.

They took a holiday in a tin bus and bowled along on the Chinese mainland through Canton. For miles the road was lined with rusty factories all dropping to bits. 'These were sold to us by the Russians,' said their guide. 'We were conned.' In the shadows of the rusted chimneys lay wide stretches of murky water sometimes with lotuses. White ducks floated among the lotuses on the foul olive-green water. The road was terrible, full of gritty holes, narrow and mean. Tall factories trailed hundred-foot stripes of mould down their sides, like dark green seaweed. All the small windows were boarded up.

The bus stopped for photographs and most people got out and stood in a row looking down on men scratching the surface of fields. The cameras clicked. The men were so thin you could see their bones under their belted cotton blouses. Their hats were the immemorial lampshades, colourless and beautiful. 'Make sure you get the hats in,' shouted the photographers. The fieldworkers continued to drag their sticks along the soil and never once looked up.

'Do they dream of Hong Kong?' said Elisabeth.

'We don't know what they dream of.'

The bus lurched on and the guide beseeched them to look to the right, at the distant and very modern restaurant where they would be stopping for lunch. 'On no account look *left*. Do not look *left*.'

Everybody looked left to where a ragged column of men in white robes and pointed hats jogged along the side of a field. Several of them carried a bundle tied to a pallet on long poles.

'It's a funeral,' said Betty. 'To see a funeral means bad luck.'

'That's a Chinese funeral,' shouted another tourist on the bus. 'Or it's the Ku Klux Klan.'

The driver rattled on down the winding road and up the track to the restaurant. Someone shouted, 'Isn't it bad luck to see a Chinese funeral?'

'I saw no funeral,' said the guide. 'What funeral?'

A very old English couple held hands, without looking at each other. 'We were born here,' they said. 'We've been away a long time.' 'I was born in Tiensin,' said Betty. 'I grew up in Shanghai.' They looked at her and nodded acknowledgement. 'We are displaced people,' said the old woman, and Filth said, 'I suppose you didn't know Judge Willy?' 'What, old Pastry? Of course we did,' and they all smiled. 'When Pastry Willy was born, you know, there was only one godown in Hong Kong.'

The bus reached a town where they all got off and went

into a big store where the tourists began to run about excitedly, buying ceramic vases and teapots and enormous electric table lamps with Chinese scenes running round them, half the price of Hong Kong and a tenth of the price of Harrods. Filth asked Betty if they wanted a new table lamp. 'No,' she said, 'not these,' and was astonished to find that an image had appeared among the chinoiserie of a heavy brass oil lamp with a globe and chimney, and a thick white cotton wick. As she looked, the misty globe cleared and a flat blue flame appeared along the wick. It bounced up violet, then yellow, becoming steady and clear. A wisp of blue rising from the chimney. Betty stretched towards it and her hand passed through nothing.

'What are you doing?' asked Filth.

'I don't know. Having a vision or something. Some sort of memory thing. It must be because of those old expats finding their own country. Let's go back to the bus. There's absolutely nothing for us here.'

Back in Hong Kong she said, 'Filth – have we made up our minds? Will we be retiring here?'

He said, 'I don't intend to retire at all. I've masses still to do.'

'You'll soon be over seventy.'

'I'm a better judge the older I get.'

'You all say that.'

'I'll get the hint if they want me to retire.'

'So you're just going to sit in judgement in a dying colony for the rest of your life?'

'If you must know, I've been asked to take a break and write up the Pollution Laws. It will be internationally important.'

'They have actually approached you, then?'

'Yes.'

'Oh, well, congratulations. When would I have been told? You know what they'll say?'

'Yes. "Filth on Filth". I'm not stupid.'

'Sometimes I think there's a wit at work in the Lord Chancellor's Office, unlikely as they look to be. They choose you for your dotty names. Like "Wright on Walls".'

He nearly said, 'Next will be "Veneering on Shams",' but didn't.

'I feel quite honoured, as a matter of fact,' he said. 'And another thing, I've been chosen to rewrite *Hudson*.'

'Who on earth is Hudson?'

'We've been married for a thousand years and you don't know *Hudson*!'

'Only his Bay.'

'How very amusing. Ho-ho. *Hudson on Building Contracts*. I dare say I'll get a knighthood.'

'How thrilling. But couldn't you do this anywhere?'

'Well, London would be easiest. Or Oxford. The Law Library. Cambridge, maybe, but I'm not from that quarter. But, well, bit of a harsh old-age after here. No servants. No decent weather. Holidays in the Lake District. Cold. Raining. All these groups of singing boys strumming out rubbishy songs. And the food!!'

'Yes,' she said. 'The food. But there's opera as well as The Beatles, and there's the London theatre and concerts.'

'Everyone talks about going to the theatre and concerts, but how many of us actually go? And London's not England any more. We'd be just another old couple.'

'We could look around. It's twenty years since we went anywhere in England except London. We could go and look up Dulcie and Pastry Willy. Willy must be getting on a bit now. In Dorset.'

That same night, at the end of the Long Vacation and the trip to Canton and three months since the execution, Betty heard Filth yelling in his sleep and ran into his room. He woke, moaning, saying that they were going to hang him. After the handover in '97 they would take him and hang him.

The following morning, neither of them mentioned the night and he was driven smoothly in to Court as usual, but Elisabeth began to make plans for England and wrote one of her sketchy letters to Willy in the Donheads of Dorset.

Dear Dulcie and dear Willy
    We are coming back to see England again for a while, and we would so much like to see you in particular. Time has not passed. We so often think of you. Christmas cards are not enough.
    Could you write and say if you will be about around Christmas? Could we spend a night or so with you, or could you find us somewhere? We won't stay long because we'll be exploring. We don't quite know what to do with our future.

With best love, as ever
Betty (once Macintosh of Shanghai)
PS How are your children? Have you grandchildren?

Chapter Twenty-six

Two profiles, one imposed against the other, like images of royalty upon a medallion struck for a new reign: Edward Feathers and his wife Elisabeth, motoring into the sunset on the A33 through Wiltshire on a frosty winter's afternoon.

They were looking for Pastry Willy and Dulcie, and wondering if there would be anything to say after so long.

'Didn't they have some children?' Betty said. 'A girl. She must be quite ancient now.'

'No. Born very late. Still young. Susan.'

'Oh, lawks yes,' said Elisabeth. 'Sullen Susan.'

'Sullen Sue,' said Filth. 'I'm glad we have no sullen daughter.'

She said nothing. They were passing Stonehenge.

'We turn off quite soon. Just past Stonehenge. There's Stonehenge.'

He drove on, not turning his head. She made the sign of the Cross. Still not turning his head, Filth said, 'What on earth are you doing?'

'Well, it's the usual thing to make the sign of the Cross

passing Stonehenge. There are thousands of accidents. It's the magnetism of the stones.'

He said, after a time, 'I sometimes wonder where you hear these things.'

'It's common knowledge.'

'There are accidents because drivers all say "There's Stonehenge – look!" and turn their heads. I have a certain amount of sense.'

'Well, then, quick! Turn left. Here's the road to Chilmark. You nearly skidded! It's much narrower. And winding. Oh, look at that tree. It's enormous. It's just like a hen!'

'A hen?'

'Like a huge hen nodding on a nest. Up at the top of a tree – we've gone under it now.'

'A hen in a *tree*?'

'Yes. And I've seen it before.'

'Very unlikely. We've not been here before.'

'I came down here alone once. After that operation. It was somewhere here. Somewhere.'

'No, that was much further west. I know. I came and found you. It was near Somerset. It was way beyond Bath. Near the theatre and those Dickensian people you liked then.'

'I suppose so,' she said. 'We couldn't find them either. We never saw them again. Did we?'

'Well, didn't they die?'

'I suppose – I can't remember if we heard or not. I did write. I sent them a replacement of something I broke. I can't remember . . .'

A very old man appeared out of the hedge and crossed the road in front of them. He was carrying an axe.

'Elisabeth – what is it now?'

'I don't know. I just have the feeling I've been here before. A shuddering.'

'When people say that,' said Edward, 'nobody ever knows what to reply, like when they tell you their dreams. Here's a notice saying "The Donheads", whatever they are. St Ague is the one we're after. "*Ague*" – what a name! Here's the hill marked on the map she sent. It could be quite soon now. What a maze.'

'I think it's to the left. No, we've passed it. It was that double driveway, wasn't it, dividing left and right? Down and up.'

'No,' he said. 'We have to pass a church first. It says on the map. Here's a church. Here's Privilege Lane. Oh, yes indeed! *Very* nice! Trust old Willy! Wrought-iron gates! – oh,' and '*Hello* Willy! What a marvellous place!'

(Mutual exclamations of joy and Willy at once takes Elisabeth up and away from the house to the top of the garden and Edward takes the luggage while Dulcie goes to make one of her soufflés.)

'What a view, what a view, Willy! What a white and golden view! And Uncle Willy, we'll *never* call you Pastry any more. You're brown as a nut. It must be Thomas Hardy.'

'Thomas Hardy was always going up to London to the theatre but I never leave the Donheads,' and he began to totter back to the house, Elisabeth pretending that she needed his arm when they both knew that he was needing hers. He said, 'We have a surprise for you. Two surprises. One is Fiscal-Smith.'

'Oh, Willy, no! How *could* you?'

'Motoring through looking for a cheap bed and breakfast, he says. Then, miraculously, remembering us.'

'But have you room for us all? You said Eddie and I could stay with you tonight.'

'Yes. Of course. Vast great place, this, in spite of the thatch and the button windows. Someone else is staying, too. Our second surprise: Susan. From Massachusetts. She says she's not seen you since she was at school.'

'No. She hasn't. Is she alone?'

'Don't ask. Husband trouble in Boston. She's walked out on him and the child. She doesn't say much. We just let her thump around the countryside on a local horse. We're used to it. Always doing it.'

'Oh, I'm so sorry, Willy.'

'Aha – there's Fiscal-Smith at the front door! The wedding party is complete.'

The table in the palatial cottage was laid for a pre-war, middle-class English afternoon tea. There were dozens of postage-stamp sandwiches, brown and white bread and butter (transparent), home-made jams and seed cake. Dulcie sat behind a silver teapot.

Susan, however, was crouched in a corner on a rocking chair near the fire and her baleful eyes surveyed them. She had a mug of tea in one hand and was barefoot. As Betty and Filth came into the room her mouth was wide open ready to receive the slice of cake that was approaching it via her other hand.

'Susan,' cried Elisabeth, as was required.

'Oh, hullo.'

Filth nodded curtly. He was surprised to find her familiar, and a shadow from his schooldays passed before his eyes. Another girl at someone's house during the war. Isobel Ingoldby. Tall Isobel, with her loping golden beauty, and her dark moods. He had thought that women were less disagreeable now. He watched this one bleakly. Oh, thank God for Betty.

Everyone sat down.

Later came dinner, and Susan ate from a private menu. Again, for Filth, the great wave of memory and – well, actually – desire.

The next day Susan was not about at breakfast but passed the window later upon a steaming horse, not turning her head.

Fiscal-Smith left early. He was aiming to drop in on another old colleague, known to have a spare bedroom, who lived near York. 'Have you looked around up there, Filth? Decided where to settle? You are coming Home, I hope? It would be good to have you nearby.'

But were they coming Home? They had certainly worked at it. Filth had prepared an itinerary as thoroughly as he had done for their expeditions to Java and Japan during Bar vacations. They had borrowed a tiny flat in the Temple as a base, hired a good car, bought maps and guidebooks and set forth anticlockwise, up the Great North Road (now called the A1) and much faster than it used to be. They bypassed Cambridge because it was so cold and not Oxford, and proceeded towards East Anglia which seemed colder still, and windy. They stayed a night with a delightful ex-judge who had taken up poetry and market gardening. They met his friends who were all, it seemed, growers of kale. They explored the eastern seaboard but Filth found the sea colourless and threatening, and Betty found the glittering churches too big for flower arrangements.

They drove on, up to York which was impersonal and then up to the Roman Wall where they had Hong Kong friends whose bodies and minds had shrivelled against the climate. Approaching the Border country, they surveyed Scotland across the lapping grey waters of the Solway. 'If our genes are here,' said Filth, 'we ought at least to give Scotland a try.'

So they stayed at a grand hotel on Loch Lomond and visited another retired lawyer from the Far Eastern circuit, Glasgow-born and seeming ashamed of ever having been away. He was full of a Case to do with some local mountains that had been stacked with warheads in the Seventies. They were all there, *oh* yes. He himself was not for Aldermaston. Always good to have defences. Bugger the Russians. They wondered if his mind had been touched, perhaps by radiation.

They stepped back from Scotland like people on the brink

of a freezing plunge without towels, and turned south-east towards the Lake District and Grasmere because Betty had liked Wordsworth at school. Pilgrims queued outside Dove Cottage and the lakeside was thick with Japanese. They felt foreigners.

'There must be something wrong with us,' she said. 'We are jaundiced has-beens,' and they stopped off at a roadside pub as pretty as a calendar to think about it. The pub was just outside the delectable little town of Appleby. It was 1.30 p.m. and they asked for lunch. '*This* time of day?' said the proprietor. 'Dinner here's at twelve o'clock! *Sandwiches*? You can't ask him to make sandwiches after one o'clock. He needs his rest.'

So back south. They agreed, unspokenly, not to look at Wales where Filth had suffered as a child, nor Lancashire and west Cumberland where at his prep school – though they never talked about it – they both knew he had been unbelievably, almost unbearably, happy. A time sacred and unrepeatable.

Down the M6 they drove, and the air warmed. They spent a night in Oxford but did not look anybody up. (Too cliquey. Too long ago.) They drifted south towards Pastry Willy. And, for Betty, a dream garden that had probably never existed. She didn't explain this. She wore new armour now.

And then the hen in the tree and a man with an axe.

Before they left Privilege Hill Betty said, 'I've remembered, the place I stayed when I was convalescing was called

Dexters. At least the people were called Dexter. D'you remember them? From Ebury Street? They were actors.' But Dulcie and Willy, waving from the wrought-iron gate, said there was nobody they'd heard of called Dexter in the Donheads.

'Goodbye,' they all called out to each other. 'Thank you. Oh! How we'll miss you,' and Willy took Elisabeth's bright sweet face between his hands and kissed it.

Susan went back to Boston the following week and, leaving, said, 'Those Feathers – I can't stand them. Never could. So bloody *smug*. And politically *ignorant*. And culturally *dead*! And childless. And selfish. And *so* bloody, bloody *rich*.'

'Elisabeth', said Dulcie, 'wanted ten children.'

'Oh, they all say that. Posh brides with no brains.'

'Elisabeth has brains,' said Willy. 'She was at Bletchley Park in the war, decoding ciphers, and Filth passed out top in the Bar Finals. And they're neither of them posh!'

'Dry as sticks,' said Susan.

'No,' said Willy.

'Wasn't there some sort of scandal about *her*?' Susan's eyes gleamed.

'*No*,' said Willy.

'Oh, well,' said Susan. 'Her memory's not much. There's a house called Dexters here in the village. I passed it out riding. It's down that lane that divides. One up, one down. You can't see it from the road.'

'Oh, nonsense, we'd know it.'

'The Dexter place, all you can see is down its chimney unless you go round to the front entrance, down the hill, towards Donhead St Anthony. It's been a ruin for years. I asked because it's being all done up.'

'Darling, why didn't you *tell* them?'

'Why should *they* live here? I can't.'

So the Feathers settled down for a London winter in the Temple, Filth working on his Pollution Bill, excellent Sunday lunches in the Inner Temple Hall after church, theatres, old friends and an occasional weekend in Surrey. They grew dull. Filth went back to Hong Kong for a while, but Betty stayed behind.

Old Willy died in the New Year and Betty asked Dulcie to stay with her in the flat, which was close to the Temple church where the memorial service would be held. Betty had gone to the funeral of course, in the Donheads, and seen Willy lowered into the Dorset soil in his local churchyard. Susan had not come from America but she would be at the memorial service. Betty invited her to stay with her in the Temple, too, but this was left uncertain. Which is to say that Susan did not reply.

Oh, well, thought Elisabeth.

It was a splashy, showery day and the congregation arrived shaking umbrellas and stamping their wet shoes in the porch of the Temple church. Willy had been so contentedly old, they were all telling each other, that this was a celebration of his life, not a lament. There were a few old lawyers from Singapore and Hong Kong and some Benchers from all the Inns of Court who faced each other sanguinely across the chancel, occasionally raising a hand in greeting.

Betty sat wanting Filth there. She felt very sad. Dulcie next to her was perfectly dressed in Harrods black with a glint of Chanel, eyes streaming, and sulky Susan was gulping and snuffling into a big handkerchief. Betty hadn't bothered much with what to wear or whom to greet. She sat thinking of Willy and old Shanghai and nursery rhymes a thousand years ago. I do know love when I see it, she thought. He loved me and I loved him. Nobody much left. And she tried to ignore the hatchet face, directly across from her, of Fiscal-Smith in a black suit worn slippery with funerals.

There was a scuffle and commotion and, across the church, Fiscal-Smith made room ungraciously for a stumbling latecomer who was nodding left and right in apology. The Master of the Temple was already climbing to the pulpit to read from the Holy Bible. The latecomer looked at Betty across the chancel, directly head-on to him, and gave a delighted wave. It was Harry Veneering.

'Come on out to tea,' he said afterwards.

They were all gathering outside the church or crammed into the porch, and some had begun to walk over the courtyard to the wake in Parliament Chamber. It was not quite raining but damp, and many of them were old. The senior Benchers were filing away from the church through their private door under umbrellas, and Dulcie and Susan were being cared for by the Master of the Temple.

'Come on, don't go that way,' said Harry Veneering to Betty. 'Come with me round here past these gents on the floor,' and he took her elbow and led her away among the circle of Knights Templar on their tombs, swords in place. Chins high.

'Promising juniors who didn't quite make it,' said Harry. 'I'd have been the same if I'd gone to the Bar. The Army was for me. Mind, the Army didn't seem to do them a lot of good, proud bastards pretending to be like Jesus. Killing everybody. Taxi!'

'Where are we going?'

'The Savoy.'

'But it's only a two-minute walk.'

'We're not walking. I'm an Officer in the Brigade of Guards.'

'And', she said, 'we haven't booked.'

'Oh, they'll find me a table.'

He gave the saluting doorman a wave, and took her through the foyer laughing and smiling around. Yes, *of course*, sir, a table. No, of course not, sir. Not too near the piano. They sat in an alcove where lamplight and warmth denied the soggy day.

'Yes,' he said, '*full* afternoon tea and, *yes*, the glass of champagne. Naturally. And –' he looked at her and took her hand.

'Harry, stop this at once. They'll think you're my – what is it called? – toy boy!'

'Oh, but I *am*,' he said. 'Mrs Waterproof and galoshes! Hey – look at my right thigh!' He stuck out his leg just in front of the approaching waitress, and there were shrieks and laughter.

'Harry – *will* you sit down. You're no better than when you were nine.'

'I wish they served lobsters,' he said.

Shriek.

'And I wish I was under the table again, missing my plane back to school. I wish – I wish I'd never grown up.'

'Harry, how dare you! How *can* you? All we did!'

'Sorry. Yes. Look at my thigh. It's twice the width of my left one, twice as strong. Whenever I have X-rays it makes them faint. Wonderful operation. Did you read in the papers? I climbed the Eiger.'

'Yes, I did.'

'Not that I'm the first.'

'No, you're not. And how did it get in the papers?'

'I attract attention. Like my father.'

Pouring pale gold tea she said, 'And where is your father? And your mother? I thought they'd be here at the service.'

'Pa's in Fiji doing an Arbitration. I suppose Ma's at home in HK. I don't hear much from her.'

'You hear from your father?'

'Oh, yes. But I'm in his black books at the moment.'

'Why?'

'Don't go into it. Extravagance. I think he rather likes to boast about it really. Makes me seem a toff.'

'He's been very good to you.'

'So have you, Miss Raincoat. You are my true and only love. Someone told me you were with me all night long before I nearly had my leg chopped off.'

A waiter came with the champagne.

'It's true,' Harry said to him. 'She was with me all night long. Out on the Russian steppes. She stopped them amputating my leg. Then things got out of hand and we were attacked by wolves . . .'

'Will that be all, sir?'

'Oh, no!' said Harry. 'Lots more to come.'

'Harry,' she said. 'I must go back to the wake and look after Dulcie. She's staying with me.'

'Where's Hyperion?' he asked. 'Can't he look after her? Filth, I mean. Sir Edward?'

'He's abroad. He's arbitrating, too. He's retiring soon, and then we're going to live in Dorset, near Dulcie.'

But he was staring at the clock across the room. 'Good God in heaven,' he said. 'Good *God*! The time! I have to go,' and he began to pat his pockets. 'I'm dreadfully late. I – my wallet!'

'It's all right,' she said. 'I'm taking you out to tea. Next time you can give me dinner. At the Ritz.'

'I will! I'd love to. Mrs Burberry, my angel of light,' and he was gone, flitting through the room and out of the foyer through the glass doors into the Strand.

She followed after paying the huge bill and walked back to the Temple and into the sombre celebration for her dear old friend. As she came into the room she seemed to see him somewhere in the crowd watching her and lovingly shaking his head.

'I haven't a son,' she told the ghost. ('Oh, *hello*, Tony! Hello, Desmond!') 'I haven't a child. I've no one else to be unwise with. I so love him.'

Chapter Twenty-seven

Dexters was an immediate success. There was very little of the old cowman's cottage left. All had been enlarged and the garden opened widely to the view. The entrance was no longer the breakneck business of Elisabeth's first haunted visit and there was electricity, an Aga, a telephone, a splendid kitchen, two bathrooms, a dining room for the rosewood table and a hall wide enough for the red chair. And a terrace, facing the sunset for gin on summer evenings. The great stone chimney remained. Dexters was private and quiet but not so isolated that the two of them would one day become a threat to the social services when they be seriously old. There was a shop half a mile away, the paper and the groceries were delivered, as of yore, and the church stood up unchanging near Dulcie on Privilege Hill. There was a room for Filth to work in surrounded by his shelves of Law Reports, and a hidden garage for one modest car. The almost virgin – if there is such a thing – garden beckoned, and deliveries began of Betty's plants. A gardener was found, and a cleaner who also did laundry. There was the smell of leaves and dew when you opened the windows and the smell of the new wood floors within, and the wood-burning stove. Betty gathered lavender and scattered it in chests of drawers.

And so they settled. The curtains of lights and fireworks and the clamour and glamour and luxury and squalor of Hong Kong were over for them. The sun rose and set less hectically, less noticeably, but more birds sang. The rookery was still there, the nests, now huge and askew, weighing heavily in the branches, the birds – probably, said Filth, the same ones – still disputing and objecting and arbitrating and condemning, passing judgement and gathering further and better particulars. Filth said that so long as they were there he'd never miss his profession.

Memory changed for both Edward and Elisabeth. There were fewer people now to keep it alive. Christmas cards dwindled. Instead, Betty began in October to write letters to the best of those left. Not many. Amy and Isobel and a couple of dotty cousins of Edward. Just as she had rearranged herself into a copy of her dead mother on her marriage, now she began to work on being the wife of a distinguished old man. She took over the church – the vicar was nowhere – and set up committees. She joined a Book Club and found DVDs of glorious old films of their youth. She took up French again and had her finger- and toenails done in Salisbury, her hair quite often in London where she became a member of the University Women's Club. She knew she still looked sexy. She still had disturbing erotic dreams.

She quite enjoyed the new role, and bought very expensive county clothes, and she wore Veneering's pearls (Edward's were in a safe) more and more boldly and with less and less guilt.

As ever, she kept Veneering's diamond clasp round the back of her neck in the daytime and only risked it round the front at dinner parties, where sometimes it was exclaimed over. Filth never seemed to notice.

One day Filth said, 'Do you remember that I once took part in an Arbitration at The Hague?'

'The International Court of Justice? Of course I do. I didn't see you for months. You said it was dreary.'

'That fellow was on the other side.'

'Veneering,' she said. 'Yes.'

'We kept our distance. You didn't come out.'

'I did, actually. Just for a night or two. I met a schoolfriend in a park. I don't remember much. It was after we – we married.'

'*Well*,' he said, looking through his glass of red wine and tipping it about. 'I've been asked there again.'

'What! It's been years . . .'

'It's an engineering dispute about a dam in Syria. I've done a few dams in my time. The two sides have been rabbiting on, squandering millions. They want to bring in a couple of new arbitrators to sit above the present ones.'

'*Could* you? Do you want to? Aren't you rusty?'

'I could. I'd like to. I don't think so. Come too. The Hague's a lovely place, and there's so much around it. There's Delft and Leyden and Amsterdam and Bruges. Wonderful museums. Paintings. Oh, and good, clean food. Good, clean people. Good for you!'

'I'll think. But you should do it.'

'Yes. I think so. I think so.'

'The International Court of Justice! At your age.'

'Yes.'

'But', he said a week later, 'it's out of the question. Guess whom they want as the third replacement arbitrator?'

She licked her fingers. She was making marmalade.

'Easy,' she said. 'Sir Terence Veneering QC, Learned in the Law.'

'Yes.'

'Does it matter? Isn't it about time . . .?'

'Well, I suppose so!' said Filth. 'And he's the only other one who knows as much as I do about dams. It would be a fair fight. I needn't speak to him out of Court.'

'Is he "Dams"?'

'Yes. He got the Aswan Dam once. I'd have liked that one. However, I got the dam in Iran. D'you remember? It wouldn't fill up. Very interesting. They'd moved half the population of the country out and drowned all their villages. I won that. I had death threats there, you know.'

'You always thought so. Will this dam be interesting?'

'*All* dams are interesting,' he said, shocked.

*

Later, eating the new marmalade at breakfast, she said, 'But I don't think I'll come with you, Filth, my darling. If you don't mind.'

'Why not?'

'Oh, well. It's Easter. I'm needed at church. And so on.'

'Dulcie could do all that.'

'Well. No, I'm happy here, Eddie. I'm used to you being away, for goodness' sake. It's not like in East Pakistan with only three telephone lines.'

'Well, I'll go. Actually' – he gave his crazy embarrassed roar – 'I have actually accepted the job, so I'll go and I'll come back at weekends. I can be back here every Friday night, you know, until the Sunday night. And – you never know – you might change your mind and come out to me for a weekend? We could stay somewhere outside The Hague.'

So she was alone in the Donheads through the early spring. It was a bitter Lent, cold and lonely. When Eddie's car dropped him off at Dexters each Friday night and she had dinner ready for him and news of village matters, he seemed far away and unconcerned.

'Are you enjoying the International Court of Justice?'

'Well, "enjoying"? The creature is still poisonous. Still hates me. But I'm glad to be there. Betty, come out and join me. We can stay away from The Hague and all that. It's such a chance for you. Buy bulbs.'

'Oh,' she said.

'You can order a million tulips there,' he said.

'Tulips,' she said.

'Well, think about it.'

'I love you, Filth. Oh, yes, well, yes. I'll come!'

Chapter Twenty-eight

So she went. They stayed in an hotel near Delft and Edward was driven from there to The Hague and back each day, so she saw nothing of the Court.

And the tulip fields were in their glory and she booked for all the tours to see them, sometimes staying overnight, and each time ordering quantities of bulbs for Dorset, to be delivered in October. She talked ceaselessly to other gardeners on the coach tours and on the canal boats, and forgot all else.

She shopped. She bought a broadsword from an antique shop because it reminded her of Rembrandt's warrior. She bought a blue and white Delft knife with a black blade and broken handle because it might once have cut up fruit in Vermeer's kitchen. She bought three seventeenth-century tiles for Dulcie – a boy flying a kite, a fat windmill, a boat with square sails gliding through fields – and, for Amy, a heavy copper pot, trying not to think of the postage. She bought a print of a triptych for Mrs Baxter. She walked for miles – the presents were always delivered back to the hotel – down cobbled streets between tall houses and a central canal. From windows, faces looked out and nodded. These must be homes for the elderly, she thought. What shining, broad faces. They wore round white caps with flaps. She expected Frans Hals at any moment to come flaunting down the street. All just out of sight.

On the fourth Saturday morning, the day Filth usually flew home for the weekend, he had to take documents back to the Arbitration room.

He brought his locked briefcase to the breakfast table and set it at his feet and she said, 'Edward, aren't you rather overdoing it? We could just drop the papers off on the way to the airport.'

'No, I may have to talk to the other two. They'll be there.'

He was wearing his dark Court suit of striped trousers and black jacket, a sober tie, a starched shirt and Victorian silk handkerchief.

'I'm sure the others won't go dressed like that,' she said.

'I dare say not, but it's correct. I'm carrying papers.' Filth and Betty agreed to meet back at the hotel after lunch.

She took a taxi to a gallery she hadn't been to before where there were some seventeenth-century flower paint-ings, and walked round and round the sunlit rooms, empty because it was not yet the Easter holidays and there were no tourists. She felt embarrassed at the clatter of her feet in the silence and tried to tiptoe from one room to the next, the sun throwing gold stripes across the polished floors. Doors stood open between the galleries, the sun illuminating other distances, withdrawing itself from foregrounds, changing direction, splashing across a distant window or open door. Inside the building, everywhere was silent and, outside, the canal was black and still. She looked for a chair and found one standing by itself and sat down. But the gallery was disappointing. She sat looking at paintings of dead hares with congealed blood on their mouths, swags of grapes, pomegranates, feathered game collapsed sightless on slate slabs. In a corner of the room was a wooden carving, the head and shoulders of a man on a plinth, the wood so black it must have lain untouched for centuries in some bog, the cracked wood perfect for the seamed and ancient face, heavy with all the miseries of the world.

But it was the hat that informed the man. It was clearly the hat that had inspired the carving. It had a tight round crown and a cartwheel of an oak brim, biscuit-thin, spread out much wider than the stooped shoulders. The hat of a religious? A pilgrim? A wandering poet? Had it all been carved from one piece of wood? Was the hat separate? Did it lift off? She became hypnotised by the hat. She had to touch it.

She heard footsteps and a gallery attendant stood in the doorway, then passed on, his careful, slow feet squeaking.

Then she heard in an adjoining gallery two voices.

'Well, what about *me*? What am *I* to do?'

'Go back to lunch at the hotel. Or a restaurant. Go and rest. We'll be off at four o'clock.'

'I want to go to Beirut for the weekend.'

'*Beirut*! It's across the world! And it's nightclubs and narcotics. Whatever . . .?'

'I want to go for massage. Get my hair cut.'

'*Beirut!*'

'Yes. I'm bored. It's the place now. I'm going to Beirut.'

An overweight figure passed sloppily across an open doorway into a further gallery and it was Elsie Veneering. Another shadow followed, and Elisabeth heard their voices on a staircase. 'But what shall I *do* all the *afternoon*? Where shall I *go*? I can't sit having lunch alone.' Elisabeth heard a taxi drive away. She closed her eyes and listened, and very soon heard him coming back up the stairs.

He said from a distance, 'I saw you as we came in. She's gone,' and she opened her eyes on a small seedy man without much hair, feeling in his pockets for a cigarette.

She said, 'You can't smoke in here,' and he said, 'No, I suppose not.'

He was wearing blue jeans and a brown shirt. He didn't look much.

She was wearing a new long tight-fitting coat with a round fur collar and a trimming of the same fur down the front, disguising the buttons, and then circling the hem. It gave her a young waist and legs. Her hair had been cut in Amsterdam. He said, 'You are much more beautiful now. But I loved your looks then, too.'

They sat in silence, he across the room on the only other chair. They looked at one another, and his smile and his eyes were as they had always been.

He said, 'This bugger in the hat, he's like that dwarf who, history relates, nicked Filth's watch when they were kids and sold it,' and he got up and whispered in the man's oak ear, 'Albertross – I gotcher!' and lifted the wide oak brim and shouted out, 'Eureka! It's a separate entity!'

And dropped it. She screamed.

He said, picking it up, 'It's OK. It's bog oak. Seventeenth-century, harder than iron. Oh, and the bloke's name is Geoffrey. It says so in the label: "Bought at Harrods".' He crammed the hat back on the head and the attendant came back and stared as Veneering bent to the oak ear, disarranging the hat, and said, 'Hush, be still.' He crossed to the attendant and shook hands with him. 'It's my grandfather. He was a hatter. Rather a mad one. Nothing's broken,' and the man went quickly away.

'No, I'm not laughing. I'm not,' she said, 'I'm not. I'm not.'

And he took her hands and said, 'When did you last laugh like this, Elisabeth? Never – that's right, isn't it? We've messed our lives. Elisabeth, come away with me. You're bored out of your head. You know it. I know it. And I'm in hell. It's our last chance. I'll leave her. It was always only a matter of time.'

But she got up and walked out and down the circular staircase, the water from the canal flashing across the yellow walls. He leaned over the rail above, watching her, and when she was nearly down she stopped and stood still, not looking up.

'You're not wearing the pearls.'

She said, 'Goodbye, Terry. I'll never leave him. I told you.'

'But I'm still with you. I'll never leave you. We'll never forget each other.'

On the last step of the staircase she said, 'Yes. I know.'

Chapter Twenty-nine

All that summer Elisabeth gave herself to the garden. Dexters as a house was now perfect. Its terrace had been built to sit out and eat on in warm weather. The warmth of autumn and winter was beginning to be talked about, and the fact that there was no need now to escape to winters abroad. Filth sat for hours watching Elisabeth toil.

'I sit here and bask,' he said, 'I am shameless. But she won't let me anywhere near, you know. If I pull out a weed she screams and says she'd been keeping it for the Chelsea Flower Show. All I do is wash up and pour out drinks. Oh, and I can occasionally hold a hosepipe.'

Filth's last Case, the dam at The Hague, had groaned its way to a close. The judging was over and done, and the terrace was now his stage. He worked at *Hudson on Building Contracts*, sat reading long and hard, mostly biographies of heroes of empire, and bird books. He kept binoculars at his elbow though he seldom picked them up. Each morning he read the *Daily Telegraph* wondering which political party he belonged to and hating them all. He wished Betty would discuss it with him. Or anything with him. In the evenings she sat yawning over seed catalogues, and he often had to wake her up to go to bed. On Fridays they drove in to Salisbury to the supermarket and ate a modest lunch at the hotel. Every second month a crate of wine was delivered to Dexters by Berry Brothers of St James's. On Sundays at half past ten was church. They never missed and never discussed why. 'We are hedonists,' he told friends. 'The last of our kind. No chores. We are rich, idle, boring expatriates and fewer and fewer people come to see us. Have a glass of Chablis.'

The year passed. The Handover took place in Hong Kong and they watched every minute of it on television. They discussed the Governor and his three beautiful daughters as if they were their own family, and when the daughters were seen to weep, Betty and Filth wept too. They watched the Union Jack come down for the last time.

'We're getting a bit senile,' he said, and she went out to the garden and began to turn the compost with a fork.

She stayed outside for hours, and Filth had a try at preparing supper and broke one of the Delft dishes. They had a wakeful night in their separate bedrooms and were only just asleep when the rooks started up at dawn.

'I'm going up to London next week,' he said. 'There is a Bench Table at the Inn. I can stay overnight with someone or other.' (They had long since given up the flat.) 'Or we could go together. Stay at an hotel. See a show.'

'Oh, I don't think so . . .'

'You're getting stuck, Betty.'

'No, I'm making a garden. We'll open for Charity next year.'

'I don't know what you think about hour after hour. Day after day. Gardening.'

'I think about gardening,' she said.

'Well,' he told Dulcie in the lane, 'I suppose this is being old. "All passion spent" – Shakespeare, isn't it?' and Dulcie pouted her pink lips and said, 'Maybe.'

After Filth had set off to London, Dulcie went round and found Betty, brown as a gypsy, busy with the first pruning of the new apple trees.

'Does that gardener do *nothing*?'

'He does all the rough.'

They sat over mugs of coffee on the terrace, staring down the wandering lawn towards the new orchard and out to the horizon and Whin Green. Dulcie said, 'Are you sure you're well, Betty?'

'Fine, except for blood pressure, and I've always had that.'

'You don't say much, any more. You seem far away.'

'Yes, I'm a bit obsessive. I'll be going on gardening out-ings in coaches before long with all the other village bores. Look, I must get on. I'm working ahead of frost.'

'Who are those people in the garden?'

'What people?'

'I saw some children. A boy and a girl. And a man.'

'Oh, yes. It's a garden full of surprises.'

One day, deep beyond the meadow grass, beyond the orchard and the apple hedges, on her knees and planting broad beans, she saw two feet standing near her hands. They were Harry Veneering's.

'Harry!'

He was delighted when she shrieked.

'I've found you, Mrs Waterproof! I heard Filth was up in London. Thought you might be lonely.'

They had lunch at the kitchen table and he drank a whole bottle of wine (Filth would wonder!) and made her laugh at nothing. As ever. He mentioned his father.

'Does he know you're here?'

'No. I'm a grown-up. I'm going bald. Anyway, we're not getting on too well, the old showman and I.'

'Oh? That's new.'

'No. It isn't. He thinks I'm rubbish. He's thought so for years.' He took a flower from a jar on the table and began to pull it to bits. He kicked out at a stool.

'Harry! You may be losing your oriental hair but you're still eight. What's wrong?'

'I'm supposed to be a gambler.'

'And are you?'

'Well, yes, in my own small way. He's always bailed me out. Now he says he won't. Not any more.'

'How much?' she asked.

'Never mind. I didn't come for that.'

'Of course not,' she said, watching him. Now he was picking at a pink daisy.

'Stop that!'

'Oh, sorry. Well, I'd better be going.'

'How much do you want?'

'Betty, I have not asked. I'd never ask.'

'How much do you owe?'

He slammed away from the table and looked down the garden. 'Ten thousand pounds.'

Then he pushed past her out of the back door and disappeared.

In time, she went and found him smoking in the dark alley where she had first arrived at the house, leaning against the great chimney breast. He was in tears.

'Here's a cheque,' she said.

'Of *course* I couldn't!'

'I have a lot of my own money. It's not Filth's. I spend most of it on the garden. If I'd had children it would all have been for them. I've not had a child to give it to.'

He hugged and hugged her. 'Oh, how I love you, Mrs Raincoat. How I love you.'

'Come. You must go home now. You're a long way from London and it's a nasty road. I'll walk with you to the car.'

'No, it's all right. Oh, thank you, so very, *very* much! Oh, how I . . .'

'I'll just get a coat.'

'Don't. I'm fine.'

But she insisted, and they walked together down the drive and up the hill towards the church.

'I'm just round this corner,' he said, 'and I'm going to hug you again and say goodbye. I'll write, of course. At once.'

'I'd like to wave you off.'

Very hesitantly he walked beside her round the side of

the churchyard to where his car was parked. It was a Porsche.

'You don't get a thing for one of these second-hand,' he said.

Chapter Thirty

When the Porsche was gone she turned for the house, stopping quite often and staring at the familiar things in the lane. Loitering gravely, she nodded at the old Traveller in the hedge, busy with his flail. (He must be a hundred years old.) He stopped hacking at the sharp branches and watched her pass and go towards the front door.

Inside it on the mat lay a letter which must have been wrongly delivered somewhere else first because it was grubby and someone – the Traveller? – had scrawled *Sorry* across the envelope. It had come from Singapore to her, care of Edward's Chambers. Though she had scarcely seen his handwriting – once on the card with the pearls so many years ago – she knew that it was from Veneering.

There was a half-sheet of old-fashioned flimsy airmail paper inside signed *THV* and the words: *If Harry comes to see you do not give him money. I'm finished with him.* She threw it into the wood-burning stove. Then she went into the garden and began clearing round the new fruit trees, toiling and bashing until it was dark.

*

'Hello?' Filth stood on the terrace.

'You're back! Already. There's not much for supper.'

'Doesn't matter. London's all eating. Come in. You can't do much more in the dark.'

'I've made a vow today,' he said. 'I'll never work in London again. I can do *Hudson* just as well at home, with a bit of planning of references. I am tired of London which means, they tell me, that I am tired of life.'

'Possibly.'

'Which makes me think that you and I ought to be making our Wills. I'll dig them out and revise them and then we'll make a last trip to London, to Bantry Street, and do the signing.'

'All right.'

'Could we go up and back on the same day, d'you think? Too much for you?'

'No, I don't think so.'

And he began to make meticulous revisions to his Will and appendices of wishes. Did she want to read it? Or should he look over hers?

'No, mine's all straightforward. Most of it to you and Amy. If you die first it will all go to Amy's children.'

'Really? Good gracious! Right, we'll get on with it then. Take three weeks – getting the appointment and so on, I'd think. We want everything foolproof.'

So the appointment was made for 3.30 p.m., on a November afternoon, which was rather late in the day for the two-hour journeys, one up and one down. The new young woman at the firm was excellent and therefore very busy. Never mind.

But getting ready on the day took longer now, even though shoes were polished and all their London clothes laid out the night before. Betty had seen to it that their debit cards and banknotes, rail cards, miniature bottle of brandy (for her dizziness) and the tiny crucifix left to her by Mrs Baxter were all in her handbag, along with the pills for both of them (in separate dosset boxes) in case for any reason they should need to stay overnight.

Filth was still upstairs, fighting with cufflinks, Betty, ready in the hall, sitting in the red chair, and the hall table beside her was piled up with tulip bulbs in green nets. They had smothered the telephone and Filth's bowler hat. There'd be a roar about that in a minute. ('Where the hell –?') She fingered the tulip bulbs through their netting, thinking how sexy they felt, when the telephone began to ring. She burrowed about under the bulbs to find the receiver and said, 'Yes? Betty here,' knowing it would be from a nervy sort of woman at her Reading Group that afternoon. Betty had of course sent apologies weeks ago.

'Yes? Chloë?'

'Betty?' It was a man.

'Yes?'

'I'm in Orange Tree Road. Where are you?'

'Well, here.'

'*Exactly* where?'

'Sitting in the hall by the phone. On the satin throne.'

'What are you wearing?'

'Wearing?'

'I need to see you.'

'But you're in Hong Kong.'

'No. Singapore. I need to see your face. I've lost it. I have to be able to see you. In the red chair.'

'Well, I'm – we're just setting off for London. Filth's putting on his black shoes upstairs. He'll be down in a minute, I'm dressed for London.'

'Are you wearing the pearls?'

'Yes.'

'Touch them. Are they warm? Are they mine? Or his? Would he know?'

'Yours. No, he wouldn't notice. Are you drunk? It must be after dinner.'

'No. Well, yes. Maybe. Did you get my note?'

'Yes.'

'I didn't tell you in it that Harry was given a medal. Twice mentioned in despatches last year. "Exceptional bravery". Northern Ireland.'

'No!'

'Hush-hush stuff. Secret service. Underground sort of stuff.'

'Should you be telling me this?'

'No. He never told us at the time. Very, very brave. I want to make it absolutely clear.'

'I believe it. I hated your letter. I saw him about a month ago and he was miserable. He said you thought he was rubbish. He didn't ask me for money. Terry? Terry, where've you gone?'

A silence.

'Nowhere. Nowhere to go. Betty, Harry's dead. My boy.'

Filth came down the stairs, looking for his bowler hat.

In the London train Filth thought: she's looking old. An old woman. The first time. Poor old Betty, old.

'You all right, Betty?'

'Yes.'

Her eyes seemed huge. Strange and swimmy. He thought, she must watch that blood pressure.

He saw how she looked affectionately at the young Tamil ticket inspector who was intent on moving them to a cleaner carriage in the first class. She was thanking the boy very sweetly. 'Perfectly all right here,' said Filth, but Betty was off down the aisle and into the next carriage. Silly woman. Could be her grandson. Still attractive. You could see the bloke liked her.

At Waterloo they parted, Filth to lunch in his Inn at the Temple, Betty he wasn't sure where. The University Women's Club right across towards Hyde Park? Whoever with? And why was she making off towards Waterloo Bridge? The solicitor's office was in Holborn. He watched her almost running down the flight of steps, under the arches and over the maze of roads towards the National Theatre. Still has good legs, bless her. He stepped into a taxi.

Betty, at the National Theatre, made a pretence of eating lunch, pushing a tray along in a queue of people excited to have tickets for *Electra* in an hour's time. She headed for the foyer (*Harry is dead*) and got the lift up to the open-air ter-race where there were fire-eaters and mummers and people being statues and loud canned music played. (*My boy Harry.*) Beside her on the seat two young lovers sat mute, chewing on long bread rolls with flaps of ham and salad hanging out. When they had finished eating they wiped their hands on squares of paper and threw the paper down. Then in one simple movement they turned to face each other and merged into each other's arms.

She decided to go at once to Bantry Street. If she walked all the way she would arrive just about on time. On Waterloo Bridge, once she had climbed the steep concrete stairs the crowds came down on her like the Battle itself. She kept near the bridge's side, sometimes going almost hand over hand. People in London move so fast! (*Harry is dead.*) Some of them looked her over quickly as they passed, noticed her pearls, her matching coat and skirt. The silk blouse. The gloves. I'm antique. They think I'm out of Agatha Christie. (*Is dead!*) My hair is tidy and well cut, like the woman . . . the woman in . . . the woman like my mother in the hairdresser in Hong Kong. The day the crowds of shadows were to pass me in the night towards the house in the trees. *He is dead*.

At the Aldwych she felt dizzy and found a pill in her handbag and swallowed it, looking round to see if by any chance Filth was anywhere about. He'd be in a fury if he couldn't find a taxi. He'd never get a bus. He wouldn't much care to walk. No sign.

Oh, but why worry? He always could find taxis. He was

so tall. Taller still when he brandished the rolled umbrella. He'd forgotten the bowler hat, thank goodness. It was still under the tulips. The last bowler hat in London and my boy is dead.

Here was Bantry Street and there, thank God, was Filth getting out of a taxi and smiling. The driver had got out and was holding open the door for him. Filth looked somebody. His delightful smile!

But it was the last smile of the day. On the next train back to Tisbury they sat opposite one another across a table in a determinedly second-class carriage. Betty was pale and Filth sat purple in choleric silence.

The solicitor had not been there! She had children ill at home and either had not remembered or the firm had forgotten to cancel the appointment. And at the reception desk – and the place looked like an hotel now, with palms in pots – they had not even seemed apologetic.

'*Salisbury*,' he said, after an hour. 'We'll take the damn things into Salisbury to sign. Perfectly good solicitors there and half the price.'

'I always said so.' Betty closed her eyes. (*Harry.*)

'It is a positive outrage. I shall write to the Law Society.' (*My boy*, *Harry.*)

'We are, after all, no longer young.'

'No.'

'Nor are we exactly nobodies. They've been our solicitors for forty years, that firm.'

'Yes.'

She opened her eyes and watched Wiltshire going by. On the way out she had thought that she'd seen a hoopoe in a hedge. Filth would have been enchanted but she had not told him. *Very brave. Despatches. Northern Ireland. Harry. No, no. He is not dead. My Harry.*

And, seeing the first of the chalk in the rippling hills she knew that she would leave Filth. She had to go to Veneering.

Filth now closed his eyes and, opposite him, she examined his face. He looked like a fine portrait of himself, each line of his face magnificently drawn. Oh, such conceit! Such self-centredness! Such silliness and triviality! I'll tell him when we get home. And a wonderful lightness of heart flooded over her, a squirm of ancient sexual pleasure.

It will probably kill him, she thought. But I shall go. I may tell him at once. Now.

The train had begun to slow down for Tisbury Station. It usually stopped just outside for several minutes, for the platform was short and they had to wait to let the fast London-to-Plymouth train through. Betty looked out of the window and on the tapering end of the platform, way beyond the signal and just as they were sliding to a halt, she saw Albert Ross. He was looking directly at her.

Filth was standing up, ready to get out. He came round to her and shook her shoulder. 'Betty. Come along. We're here. Whatever's wrong now?'

'Nothing,' she said.

In the car that they had parked outside the station that

morning but a thousand years ago, she said, 'I saw Albert Ross. Standing on the platform. Waiting for the train from Plymouth to go through.'

Filth was negotiating Berrywood Lane – a tractor and two four-by-fours, two proud girls on horseback – and said, 'You fell asleep.'

'No. He looked straight at me.'

There, on the hall table, lay the tulip bulbs.

I'll wait till I've planted them, she decided. I can't leave them to shrivel and rot, and she took off her shoes and climbed the stairs to bed. I'll tell him tomorrow after lunch.

She was up early, not long after dawn, and ready in her gardening clothes. She would change later, after she had packed. It was a damp, warm day, perfect for planting and she arranged the bulbs in groups of twenty-five for lozenge-shaped designs each in a different colour along the foot of the red wall. The planting round the apple trees was finished already. With her favourite long dibble, she began to make a hole for each bulb. She liked to plant at least six inches down. Then you could put wallflowers on top of them to flower first, but this year she had left it a bit late for that. She humped herself about on the planting mat, put a little sharp sand in the bottom of each hole, laid a bulb ready beside each. How stiff and cumbersome her body was now. How ugly her old hands, in the enormous green gloves. A hectic sunlight washed across the garden and she went into the house for a mug of coffee. Edward was in the kitchen, silent in his own world.

'Bulbs finished yet?'

'Not quite.'

She went back to the garden and he followed her, carrying his stick and binoculars on to the terrace. She stood with her coffee, and all at once the rooks started a wild tumult in the ash trees: some dreadful disagreement, some palace revolution, some premonition of change. They began to swoop about above the branches and their ramshackle great nests, all over the sky, like smuts flying from a burning chimney. She was down the garden on her knees again now and saw that Veneering's pearls were lying in the flower bed beside her. For the first time in her life she had forgotten to take off a necklace when she went to bed. Nor had she noticed them when she washed and dressed this morning. They must have slipped from her neck. She was eye to eye with them now, on her haunches, head down. She picked them off the soil and let them pour into one of the holes for the tulips.

My guilty pearls, she thought. I hope the sharp sand won't hurt them.

She had rather seized up now. She was in a difficult position on hands and knees. If I can get on my elbows . . . she thought. Goodness –! Here we go. Well, I never was exactly John Travolta. That's better. Now the bottom half.

She rested, and from her lowly place noticed out on the lawn how the bindweed was piercing the turf, rising in green spirals, pirouetting quite high, seeking something on which to cling. The wild, returning to the garden.

She could see Filth, too, sitting on the terrace with his coffee, staring up at the rooks through his binoculars. Then he put down the binoculars and picked up his Airedale-headed walking stick and, quite oblivious of her, like a child, pointed it up at the rookery and shouted, 'Bang, bang, bang.' Then he swung the stick about for a left and a right. 'Bang, bang, bang.'

He's quite potty, she thought. It's too late. I can't leave him now.

But then she did.

Filth, letting his binoculars swoop away from the rookery and down across the garden a minute later, saw her lying in the flower bed, particularly still.

PART FIVE:

Peace

Chapter Thirty-one

Three years later – the years Edward Feathers saw as his torture and suffering and the village called his fortitude – came the extraordinary news that the house next door to Dexters, the monstrous hidden house above him, had been sold.

One winter's day, a single van arrived and was quickly away again. Who had bought the upper house nobody knew. After a time Edward Feathers, on his morning constitutional to the lane end to collect his *Daily Telegraph* from the length of drainpipe attached to the rough handrail at the foot of the slope, saw that a second bit of drainpipe had been fastened to the handrail of his new neighbour across the lane. The paper was not the *Daily Telegraph*. It was thicker and stubbier, and from what he could see it was the *Guardian*.

How insolent! To copy his invention for a rainproof newspaper without his permission! He marched off on his emu legs, chin forward, plunging his walking stick into the road. He met his neighbour Dulcie, bright and smiling as usual. When he had slashed his way by she said to her dog, 'So – what's the matter with him today?'

She did not know what was to come.

About a month after the newcomer's arrival a new telephone was installed (the Donheads move slowly) and the newcomer used it to telephone the village shop in a more distant Donhead. He thanked them for the delivery of his daily paper and would the shop kindly put up a postcard in their window advertising for daily help? What was the going rate? Excellent. Double it. And stipulate laundry. The newcomer had lived in the Far East, and was ashamed to say that he was totally incapable of looking after himself.

'Oh, dear me,' they said. 'And no wife, sir?'

'My wife is dead. She was Chinese. I'm afraid she had no idea how to do laundry either. We had servants.'

'We'll do our best,' said the shop. 'You sound just like your neighbour. He was from Singapore way. He's a lawyer.'

'Oh.'

'What name shall I put on the card, sir? Perhaps you are a lawyer, too?'

'Yes, I am, as it happens.'

'Well, fancy that. You may be friends.'

'My name is Veneering.'

'Your neighbour is Sir Edward Feathers.'

There was a terrible silence. The telephone was put down. 'Funny one we've got now,' said the shop to Eddie Feathers's

248

daily who was in buying marmalade for him. 'Not a bundle of fun.'

'Makes two of them,' said Kate, and half an hour later, letting herself into the Feathers domain, 'What about this, then? Next door it's another lawyer and he's from Singapore way, too. His name's Veneering. That's a queer name if ever. Is it Jewish? He's wanting a domestic, and don't you worry, I've said I'm not available. There's enough to do here. I'll find him someone but – Sir Edward, what's wrong? You've turned greenish. Sit down and I'll get you your cup of tea.'

Feathers sat silent, stunned out of thought. At last he said, 'Thank God that Betty is dead.'

Over the way, Veneering sat on by the telephone for a long while and said at last, 'I must move. Thank God that Betty is dead.'

After a time looking at his fire, burning brightly in the great chimney, Feathers also said, 'I must move.'

A bombshell coincidence?

Yet it was really not so very unlikely that Veneering had lighted on this particular house. The Donheads are thick with retired international lawyers, and house agents' blurbs do not always mention English county boundaries. Dorset is large and, anyway, Veneering had no idea of the Feathers's address. He was not the detective his son had been. No, the only really curious thing was that after their mutual discovery, they never met. Filth, far too proud to change the route of his afternoon walk, kept to the same paths as before, went to church as before, drove to the same small supermarket as before, kept the same friends. It was Veneering who kept himself out of sight. He was, quite simply, never about. Cases of wine were delivered at quite frequent intervals, and the village shop would drop off meagre groceries on his porch up the hill. His cleaner came when she felt like it and reported that he was obviously someone 'in reduced circumstances', and his garden was left to go wild. Sometimes a hired car would come out from the station to take him to the London train and drop him at home again after dark. Later, it was reported that the circumstances could not have been that much reduced, for the hired car began to transport him all the way. When people called at the house with envelopes for Save the Children or Breast Cancer, they were ignored. The postman said he delivered very little up there. There was seldom a light.

Once, when a much younger Hong Kong lawyer called on Filth, and Filth walked him back to his car at the end of the lane, the lawyer said, 'Didn't Terry Veneering retire down this way?' before remembering the myth of the clash of the Titans. But surely over now?

'Lives next door,' said Filth.

'Next door! Then you are friends.'

'Friends?' said Filth. 'Never seen him. Certainly don't want to. That's his personal bit of drainpipe he's put up. He copied mine. He never had an original idea.'

'Good God! I've a mind to go and see him myself. He went through it, you know. This is ridiculous.'

'Go if you like,' said Filth, 'but you needn't bother to come and see me again if you do.'

Filth walked that day further than usual, and returned home after dark. It was getting towards Christmas, and Kate and the gardener had hung fairy lights around his length of lead piping. There was a holly wreath on his door and a spangle of coloured lights shone from his windows. He could see the light of his coal fire in the sitting room, a table light on in the hall showing Christmas cards standing about. As ever, the right-hand bend of the lane and the house above were in total darkness.

Don't expect he's there, thought Filth. Playboy! Probably lives half the time in his London club. Or with a whore. Or with several whores. Or in Las Vegas or somewhere vulgar for Christmas. Disneyland.

After the hellish years without Betty, Filth was, however, beginning to learn how to live again. The remorse. The loss of the sense of comfort she brought, her integration with the seasons of the year, her surety about a life of the spirit – never actually discussed. Often, when he was alone in the house and she seemed to be just at his shoulder, he would say aloud to her shadow, 'I left you too often. My work was too important to me.' He did not address the first days of their engagement though. Never. Never.

Christmases alone he liked. Positively liked. With Betty unavailable there was nobody he wanted to be with. He and Betty had gone in the last years to the hotel in Salisbury together for Christmas lunch. No fuss. No paper hats. No streamers to get caught up in all her necklaces. Now he went alone to the same hotel, the same table. Taken there and returned by taxi. Then a good read, a whisky or two before bed. This year, his fourth without her, was to be exactly as usual.

Except that it was snowing. And it had been snowing very hard since he got up. The snowflakes fell so fast and thick he could not say whether they were going up or down. He could not even see the barrier of trees that shielded him from his neighbour.

And this year – no sign of the taxi. It was already half an hour late. Filth decided to ring it up but found that his phone was dead. Ha!

He padded about – getting very late indeed now – and was relieved to hear a loud bang and slither outside in the drive. But nothing further.

Taxi's crashed against the wall in the snow, he thought, and went out of the front door one step only and still in his slippers and without his coat. But there was no taxi, only a great heap of snow that had slid from his roof into the drive. And the snow was falling faster than ever.

And behind him he heard his front door click shut on its fine Chubb lock.

And at the same moment, up behind the trees, Veneering was humped in bed, wearing a much-used fleece and his pyjamas, and thick woollen socks, under two duvets. He had examined Christmas Day with one eye, then the bedside clock with the other, groaned as he flexed his wrists and ankles, seen that his bedroom, with the old drugget on the floor and the navy-blue cotton curtains he had inherited from the farming family, was damp and dreary as usual but that round the black edges of the curtains was a suffusing, imperial dazzle. Hobbling from the bed, pulling back a curtain, he saw the snow.

The sky must be somewhere out there, too, the treetops below him, Whin Green. But all he saw was dancing snow so thick he couldn't tell if it was going up or coming down. *Coming up*, he thought, afraid. Was he still drunk from last night? *Or am I standing on my head?* He concentrated and, looking down, made out a patch of shadow, a certain darkness around – what? Yes. It must be old Filth's chimney stack, the flashing round its base on the roof. Yes. The chimney was there and a great sloppy patch of snow had melted round it and – wha-hey! As Veneering watched he saw the shadow moving and the whole slope of wetter, warmer snow (he'd have his central heating on full tilt, of course) slipped away to the ground and he heard the thunderous slap as it landed.

Kill him if he happens to be under it, thought Veneering. But I shouldn't think he is. He'll be at some ghastly party with 'all the trimmings'. He thought of Betty long, long ago sitting up very straight and perky with the paper streamers tangled up in her necklaces. Maybe sometimes his pearls . . . He was making for his bed again when the front-door bell rang.

Veneering pulled on some trousers and another fleece over the first, and something in the way of shoes, and the bell rang again. Who the hell . . .?

Looking out of his sitting-room window he saw Filth standing in his porch in a cashmere cardigan and slippers, and soaked to the skin. Very doleful face, too. Well, well. This'll kill him. Ha! The old fool's locked himself out. Went out to investigate the bang. Ha!

He answered the next peal on the bell and they confronted each other. Filth's magnificent face dropped open at the jaw like a cartoon, and Veneering remembered that he hadn't shaved. Not yesterday either. Feathers, expecting Achilles, saw a little old man with a couple of strands of yellow-grey hair across his pate, bent over with arthritis. Veneering, expecting the glory of Agamemnon, saw a lanky skeleton that might just have been dragged dripping from the sea full fathom five, and those were certainly not pearls that were his eyes.

'Oh, good morning, Filth,' said Veneering.

'Just called to say Happy Christmas,' said Edward Feathers, crossing Veneering's un-hollied threshold.

'Good of you to call,' said Veneering. 'I'll get you a towel. Better take off the pullover. I've a duffel here. And maybe the slippers? There's a fire in here.'

Together they entered Veneering's bleak sitting room where he switched on a brown electric heater in which soon a wire-worm of an element began to glow into life. 'We can put the second bar on if you wish,' said Veneering. He did so. They looked at it. 'O, *come let us be merry*,' said Veneering, 'Don't want to get mean, like Fiscal-Smith.'

A faint smile hovered round Filth's blue lips.

'Whisky?' said Veneering.

They each drank a gigantic, neat whisky. On a table lay an immense jigsaw only half finished. They regarded it, sipping. 'Too much damn sky,' said Veneering. 'Sit down.'

In a glass case on legs Filth saw a pair of chandelier earrings. He remembered them. On the mantelpiece was a photograph of an enchanting young Guards officer. The fire, the whisky, the earrings, the steady falling snow, made Filth want to weep.

'Another?' asked Veneering.

'I should really be going.'

'I was sorry to hear about Betty,' said Veneering, looking away.

'I was sorry to hear about Elsie,' said Filth, remembering her name, her beauty, her yellow silk dress at the Hong Kong Jockey Club. Her unhappiness. 'Tell me, what news of your son?'

'Dead,' said Veneering. 'Killed. Soldier.'

'I am so terribly sorry. So most dreadfully sorry. I hear nothing. Oh, I am so very sorry.'

'I sometimes think we all hear too much. It is too hard – the suffering for each other. I think we had too many Hearings all those years.'

'I must go home.'

Filth was looking troubled, and Veneering thought: in a minute he'll have to tell me that he's locked himself out. Let's see how he'll get round that.

'It was good of you to come, Filth.'

Filth said nothing for a while. Then, 'I really came to ask

you if I could use your phone. Mine's out of order. Expecting a taxi.'

(Well done, thought Veneering. Good opening move.)

'Mine will be out of order if yours is, I expect. But by all means try.'

The phone was dead.

(And the village is three miles away and the only spare key will be with his cleaner and it's Christmas and she won't be back until the New Year. And I've got him.)

'As a matter of fact,' Veneering said, 'I've meant to come and see you several times.'

Filth looked into his whisky glass. He felt ashamed. He himself had never dreamed of doing any such thing.

'Only trouble was, I couldn't think of an excuse. Bloody hot-tempered type I was, once upon a time.'

'Bloody good judge, though,' said Filth, remembering that this was true.

'You were a bloody good Advocate. Come on. One more.

'The only excuse I could think of', Veneering said in a minute, 'was that there's an old key of yours hanging up here in an outhouse. Has your address on it. Must have been here for years. Probably the last people here had been given one for emergencies. Maybe you have one of mine?'

'No, I don't think so,' said Filth.

'Shall I get it? Or some other time?'

'I may as well take it now.'

On Veneering's doorstep, the snow now thinning, wearing Veneering's unpleasant overcoat, he heard himself say, 'I

256

have a ham shank at home. Tin of crabmeat. A good bottle. If you care to come over for Boxing Day?'

'Delighted,' said Veneering.

Down the slippery slope went Filth, holding very tightly to Veneering's yews. He put the old Dexter key in the lock. Would it turn?

It did.

Chapter Thirty-two

That spring, Veneering began to play chess at Dexters once a week. Then twice a week, on Thursdays and Sundays. Each time, before he arrived, Filth moved Betty's pink umbrella from the umbrella stand in the hall to the cupboard under the stairs. Later he would bring it out again. He also moved, right out of sight, the rather magisterial photograph on the chimney piece of Betty holding up the OBE for her good works, and replaced it with one of himself and Betty laughing together in Bhutan on their honeymoon. Veneering appeared to notice nothing in the Feathers's house except the chessboard.

As the year warmed they began to meet occasionally to walk in the lanes, and Veneering grew less yellow and arthritic. He tended to stop for every passer-by for conversation and cross-examination. His charm revived, and he began again to take pleasure in everybody he met, especially if they were female. Females were always 'girls'. He used the old upper-class lingo, thought Filth. Must have learned it at embassy parties. Certainly not in Middlesbrough where he was born. Filth's snobbery was now appalling.

The 'girl' Veneering liked best was pretty Dulcie, and on meeting they would stand bobbing about in the lane together while Filth inspected the sky or sometimes pretended his walking stick was a golf club and tried out a couple of swings. They sniff round each other like dogs, he thought. Come on, Veneering, you'll catch cold.

'I begin', said Filth to Betty's shadow, 'to wish I'd left the bloody key where it was. I'm stuck with him now.'

But he was not. On one chess Thursday, Veneering said, as he took Filth's queen, 'Oh, by the way, I'm going on a cruise.'

Filth took his time. He rather interestingly shifted a knight and took Veneering's bishop. 'Oh, well done!' said Veneering. 'Yes, I'm off to the Mediterranean. Sailing to Malta. Getting some warmth into my joints.'

'I'm told it can be bitterly cold in Malta in March.'

'Oh, I'm hoping to stay with the Governor. I've met him once or twice. Nice wife.'

'You sound like Fiscal-Smith. You're not going on a cruise with him, are you?'

'Good God, no. I'm striking out.'

Filth waited to see if he'd suggest that Filth himself might accompany him. He did not.

'Betty and I found that the few expats left on Malta were pretty ropy. She called them "the riff-raff of Europe".'

'Did she? Oh, well, we're all riff-raff now. I wouldn't suggest Malta was the best place for you, Edward. Sea can be unpleasant and you're too old to fly. Insurance would be tricky.'

'I know the sea, and you are hardly younger than I am. What about *your* insurance?'

'Not bothering. I've pots of money if I catch the Maltese flu and have to go to hospital. I dare say the Governor would see me right anyway.'

Filth thought that using a phrase like 'see me right' was what he had always detested about Veneering.

The evening before he left for his cruise Veneering called on Filth with a supermarket bag full of leftovers of food that he thought Filth might like to make use of, and details of his cruise line. Filth took the leftovers into the kitchen and put them in the rubbish bin. He returned and said, 'Why?'

'Well, then someone could let me know if there was a crisis.'

'You mean you'd want to know if I should kick the bucket?'

'Well, yes, of course.'

'In order to return for my funeral?'

'Certainly not. I'd probably send the odd flower. I'd come later for your memorial service. It wouldn't be for several months, so I would be able to finish my philanderings. But yes, I'd want to know.'

Then he realised what he'd said. 'Not, of course, that I've ever been a philanderer. Never. I was always serious, which was why my life has always been so exhausting – whatever it looked like. I do know how to love a woman.'

But he was getting in deeper.

Filth sat mute. This time Veneering had gone too far. His restored health had also restored his outrageous conceit. He was still the same – *bounder* – as before.

'I'll walk home with you.'

'Oh.' Veneering hadn't planned to leave just yet. He could smell Filth's supper cooking.

'Must get my walk in before dusk,' said Filth. 'Come on,' and he took his stick from the umbrella stand where (damn) he had forgotten to remove Betty's pink umbrella. And (double damn) as, holding open the door for Veneering, he saw Veneering look at it, Bloody Hell – *touch* it!

Filth gave his queer roar. He led the way out, not to the lane end, but down his garden, past the tulip beds, the still-leafless orchard, past Betty's still-wonderful kitchen garden, her pond, her spinney, and somehow they were back at the house again but now facing the steep track that led up a bank from an alley behind a shed.

'That's the old earth closet,' said Filth. 'Come on, I'll show you a quick way home,' and he began to spring up the slippery bank like a boy.

Veneering followed on all fours.

'Good God, where are we going?'

'To the road,' said Filth. 'You'd better take my hand. When we were just a cottage there used to be an opening on the lane up here. You had to climb through – ah, come on.'

Veneering hesitated, but eventually they stood together on the upper road in the coming dark.

'I found Betty standing here once,' said Filth. 'Long ago. She'd been very ill. Somehow she found this place. To con-valesce. The station taxi brought her to this opening on the road and she stayed here all by herself. I forget for how long. It seemed very long to me. I couldn't phone. She didn't answer my letters. I was in the middle of the Reservoir Case. You'll remember it.'

'Well, you couldn't just abandon it.'

'No? Well – I wonder . . . She disappeared. Was she with you, Veneering? Not down here at all?'

'I swear to you, no. I was on the Reservoir Case, too, remember?'

'What do I remember? Didn't you leave your junior? One fantasises. I came looking for her. Found her in the end, standing here in the road in a browny-gold silk thing, soaked to the skin, her suitcase beside her. I'd been round and round, through all the bloody Donheads. Thought I'd never see her again. When I did find her, her wet face became – well, delirious with happiness. As if she saw me for the first time. And I knew I need never worry about you ever again.'

Veneering said, 'I'll get back to my packing.'

'*But*,' said Edward Feathers QC (Learned in the Law)

'– and I'll walk up with you – *but* she never knew the truth about *me*. For two nights after Betty and I became engaged to be married in Hong Kong I was with the girl who'd fascinated and obsessed me ever since I was sixteen. She happened to be passing through Hong Kong. I didn't know she knew Betty. I didn't connect her with the girl Betty was just then travelling with. I didn't even know that she and Amy and Betty were at the same school. Not until after Betty died. Then I found out that Betty and Isobel had been together at Bletchley Park, too. Betty had always called her Lizzie.

'But when I found Isobel again, there in Hong Kong, just after I'd made Betty promise never to leave me, I forgot Betty completely. For two nights I was with Isobel in my room at the Peninsular Hotel. There can't be anything more disgusting, more perfidious than that. Veneering? The only equally disgusting thing would be if some other man had that night been with Betty. Would it not?'

'It happens. This sort of thing, Filth.'

'Oh, it *happens* – but only if you are an absolute swine. Don't you think? Wouldn't you say? If you examine your meagre self? Veneering?'

'Look – it's over half a century ago. We were young men.'

'Yes. But I did something worse to Betty. I knew she wanted children. Ten, she'd said. I suspected that I was infertile. Something to do with – perhaps mumps at school. Apparently I talked to Ross – when I had fever in Africa. I can't remember any of it. Nobody knew any of it, except perhaps Isobel.

'So you see I'm not a saint, Veneering. She was worth ten of me. Yet, from the moment I found her standing here in the road I knew she would never leave me now. You were nowhere. Goodbye, old man.' And Filth walked back down the slope.

Below, beside the earth closet, Filth shouted up, 'Look, Veneering, it doesn't matter which of us was father of the child.'

'*Child!*'

'The child she lost. Before she had the hysterectomy. Yours or mine, it was not to be. What matters is to face something quite different. Betty didn't love either of us very much. The one she loved was your son. Harry.'

'Yes,' he said, his pale old face peering down. 'Yes. I believe she did love Harry.'

'Why else would she have given him ten thousand pounds?'

'That is a lie! It is a *lie*! She told me herself that Harry never asked her for money.'

Filth, despite himself, softened. 'I don't expect he did. Betty was always ready to give, whether any of us asked or not.'

So that's fixed him, thought Filth. I've won. That night he went slowly up his stairs to bed, pausing a little breathlessly on the landing. 'Checkmate,' he said.

But then, later, lying in bed, every button done up on his

264

striped pyjamas, clean handkerchief in his pyjama pocket, he wondered why he did not feel triumphant. There was no relish. No relish.

Well, he thought. That's the last I'll hear from him.

Veneering did not return from Malta. He broke one of his arthritic ankles on a stony slope where there was a deep slash in the rock masked by the night-scented stocks that grow wild all over the island and make it such heaven in the spring. A thrombosis followed, and then Veneering died.

When the news was broken to Sir Edward Feathers he said, 'Ah, well. He was a great age. He hadn't looked after himself very well. I shall miss the chess.'

About two weeks later, the Maltese postal service being so slow, a picture postcard arrived for Filth at Donhead St Ague. It said,

We are bathed in glorious sunlight here [Oh, so he got to heaven then, did he?] and I'm having a wonderfully revitalising holiday. A pity that it would have been too much for you. Today I'm going to see the one fresh-water spring on the island (life like an ever-rolling stream, etc.) with a man who says he once met you and you offered him a job as your clerk. Seems very unlikely. But memory tells all of us lies. Looking forward to our next encounter. Kind regards. T.H.V.

265

Filth did not attend Veneering's memorial service. He thought it would be theatrical to do so. The Great Rapprochement. Dulcie would tell him all about it. Kate the cleaner was a bit tight-lipped with him, saying that he could have shared a car with someone, but he said, 'I have things to see to. I am planning a journey of my own.'

'Well, I hope it's not a cruise.'

'No, no. Not a cruise. I'm thinking of going back to my birthplace for a last look round. Malaya – they call it Malaysia now, like a headache. I shall be going by air.'

She gasped and shrieked and ran to tell the gardener, and Filth saw the pair of them deep in conversation as he plodded on with *Hudson* in his study. He was negotiating about who would continue with *Hudson* when he was dead. Veneering would have been the obvious choice. Ah well.

He was beginning to miss Veneering more than he would admit. When the *For Sale* notice went up again so vulgarly in the lane it gave him a jolt. When lights of the ugly house again appeared through the trees, he was drowsing with his curtains undrawn and he woke with a start of pleasure that turned to pain as he remembered that Veneering would not be there.

'You can have anything you want of mine if I don't come back,' he had said.

Filth had said, 'Oh, nothing, thanks. Maybe the chess-men.'

*

One afternoon during a St Martin's summer, his bony knees under a tartan rug, Filth was snoozing in the garden when he became aware of a movement in one of the fruit trees and a new next-door child dropped out of it eating an apple. The child began to wander nonchalantly over the lawn as if he owned it. Filth had been reading minutes of the latest Bench Table of his Inn. He felt like throwing the child back over the hedge.

'Sorry,' the child said.

'I suppose you're wanting a ball back.'

'I haven't got a ball.'

'Well, what's that in your hand? And I don't mean my apple.'

'Just some old beads I found in that flower bed.' And he vanished.

They're so bloody self-confident, thought Filth. My prep-school Headmaster would have settled him. Then: what am I saying? Sir'd have set about teaching him something about apples.

'Keep the beads,' he called. 'They're yours.'

The night before he was to leave for his voyage home to Malaya, Filth felt such a surge of longing for Betty that he had to sit down and close his eyes. The longing had included guilt. Why guilt? Because he was beginning to forget her. Forget his long desire. 'Memory and desire,' he said aloud, 'I must keep track of them, or the game's up.' Then he thought: or maybe let them go?

There was a ring at his doorbell and a family

stood grimly on his doorstep, father, mother, son and daughter.

'Might we come in? We are from next door,' said the father (a gent, though long-haired). 'We need to speak to you on a serious matter.'

'Come in.'

They filed into the hall. 'Sebastian,' said the father, and the boy held out Betty's pearl necklace.

'He says you gave it him. We want to know the truth. He says he found it in a flower bed.'

'Yes. I did. He did. Perfectly right.' (The look in the parents' eyes. Think I'm a paedophile?)

'You see – sir,' said the father. 'We believe these pearls to be valuable.'

'Yes. I expect they are. They were my wife's. Given her by some old boyfriend. She threw them away. Silly woman. She had much better ones from me. Mine have been inherited by some cousin, I think. These – well, I'll be glad to see the last of them. Her "guilty pearls", I called them.'

'Well, really – we couldn't . . .'

'I'm just off on a trip. Look, if you want to repay me, could you just keep an eye on the house while I'm away? I have a spare key here. For emergencies.' He handed them the key that knew its way about their house. 'I hear that you are what is called "Green". And aren't you intellectuals?'

'I'm not,' said the little girl.

'Dad is,' said the boy. 'He's a poet.'

'Good, good –'

'And I'm going to do bed and breakfast,' said the wife. 'I hope you don't mind if I put up a sign on our lane?'

Chapter Thirty-three

When he stepped off the still-vibrating plane and smelled the East again, the hot airport, the hot jungle, the heavy scents of spices and humans and tropical trees and tropical food, Filth forgot everything else and knew that memory was now unnecessary and all desire fulfilled. Betty at his shoulder, he fell into the everlasting arms. The mystery and darkness and warmth of the womb returned him to the beginning of everything and to the end of all need.

His memorial service, several months later at the other side of the world, was distinguished but rather small. It was so very long since Sir Edward Feathers had been in practice. His years alone with *Hudson* had been solitary and long, and his age was so great that few lawyers could remember him as a person.

Nevertheless quite a good scattering turned up. In the Benchers' pews the Lord Chief Justice sat, for Feathers had been a great name in his time – when the Lord Chief was probably still at school. The Master of the Temple preached on Feathers's integrity and advocacy ('in a style no doubt we would now find a little dated!'), his bravery in World War Two, his long, quiet, happy marriage. His charm. He had kept clear of politics, given himself entirely to the importance of the tenets of English Law. We shall not see his like again . . . etc.

'Who's that creature?' asked one of Amy's children. Amy's grandchildren and children made quite a mob in the public pews. 'Just below the pulpit. He looks like a pickled walnut.'

Albert Ross had, in fact, been asked by an usher to move from the seats reserved permanently for Masters of the Temple but had taken no notice. Across from him in an equally regal seat in the Middle Temple Benchers' pews, a legitimate lawyer who looked preserved in aspic was glaring across at him. It was Fiscal-Smith, accompanying dear old Dulcie. He had a cheap-day return railway ticket sticking out of his pocket.

In the body of the church, across from Amy's family but a modest pew or so behind them, sat the family of Sir Edward Feathers's neighbours, the mother wearing a double string of remarkable pearls. Several pews around had filled up quite nicely with members of the Bar of the Construction Industry, particularly those from the Chambers that Sir Edward and the pickled walnut had founded. There was a clutch of clerks, one of whom had been in his pram when Sir Edward was sitting disconsolate in a draughty corridor without any work one winter's afternoon.

Then a tall and beautiful and very old woman came in and slid in beside Amy, looking at nobody. She wore a pale silk coat and her face was an enigma.

'Who's that? She's like the collarbone of a hare,' said the poet. 'I bet it was his mistress.'

They sang the usual hymns, 'I vow to thee my country' being the most inappropriate. Filth's country had never been England.

Outside afterwards, they all gathered to hear the bell toll once for every year of Filth's life, and it seemed as if it would go on for ever. It was autumn, and gold dry leaves scratched under their feet.

The dwarf, the pickled walnut, was being helped into his Rolls-Royce. He handed his large felt hat to the Chief Clerk. 'I've done with it,' he said. 'Keep it in the Chambers. It is your foundation stone.'

'Aren't you coming in to the wake, Mr Ross?'

'No. Plane to catch. I am en route to Kabul. Goodbye.' Waving a hero's wave, he was spirited away.

'Is it all a pantomime?' asked one of the children, and the poet said, 'Something of the sort.'

Inside the Parliament Chamber of the Inner Temple Hall the wine was flowing now, and the famous hat went from hand to hand. Someone said, 'He's supposed to have kept his playing cards in that hat.'

'Well, there's a zip across the inside of it.'

So they unzipped it, and found the playing cards fastened in a pouch.

'What's that other thing in there?' asked the next-door boy.

It was a small oilskin packet tied with very old string, and inside it was a watch.

Acknowledgements

My thanks to kind friends Charles and Caroline Worth, who have tried to check the topography of Hong Kong in the 1950s – an almost impossible task, and to Richard Wallington, who has answered a number of questions about the English Bar in Hong Kong. Thanks to William Mayne, for information about East Pakistan.

And gratitude to Richard Ingrams who, almost ten years ago now, asked for a Christmas story in the *Oldie* and released from somewhere in my subconscious Sir Edward Feathers QC, who has dominated three books and a large part of my life ever since. Particular thanks to my editor Penelope Hoare who has been, as ever, indispensable. Any remaining mistakes are my own.

Most of all, thanks to my husband David Gardam, especially for memories of our travels to places where the English Law continues to be heard.

Jane Gardam,
Sandwich,
Kent
2009

OLD FILTH

Jane Gardam

'A masterpiece' *Guardian*

FILTH, in his heyday, was an international lawyer with a practice in the Far East. Now, only the oldest QCs and Silks can remember that his nickname stood for Failed In London Try Hong Kong.

Long ago, Old Filth was a Raj orphan – one of the many young children sent 'Home' from the East to be fostered and educated in England. Jane Gardam's new novel tells his story, from his birth in what was then Malaya to the extremities of his old age. In so doing, she not only encapsulates a whole period from the glory days of the British Empire, through the Second World War, to the present and beyond, but also illuminates the complexities of the character known variously as Eddie, the Judge, Fevvers, Filth, Master of the Inner Temple, Teddy and Sir Edward Feathers.

ABACUS
978-0-349-11840-6

GOD ON THE ROCKS

Jane Gardam

'Tantalising, funny, sharp' *Daily Telegraph*

During one glorious summer between the wars the realities of life
and the sexual ritual dance of the adult world creep into the life of
young Margaret Marsh. Her father, preaching the doctrine of the
unsavoury Primal Saints; her mother, bitterly nostalgic for what
might have been; Charles and Binkie, anchored in the past and a
game of words; dying Mrs Frayling and Lydia the maid, given to
the vulgar enjoyment of life; all contribute to Margaret's shattering
moment of truth. And when the storm breaks, it is not only God
who is on the rocks as the summer hurtles towards drama,
tragedy, and a touch of farce.

ABACUS
978-0-349-11406-4

FAITH FOX

Jane Gardam

On page one of this novel, a dazzling young woman dies, leaving astonishment and chaos. She also leaves a new-born daughter – Faith Fox – with grandparents who belong to totally different English cultures, north and south, who speak, almost literally, different languages. Which tribe shall have her?

With wisdom, generosity and understanding, Jane Gardam takes as her subject the English heart in all its eccentric variety. *Faith Fox* sheds a clear, true light on the pain of bereavement while always offering the joyous possibility of a new beginning.

ABACUS
978-0-349-12101-7

Now you can order superb titles directly from Abacus

☐	Old Filth	Jane Gardam	£7.99
☐	God on the Rocks	Jane Gardam	£7.99
☐	Faith Fox	Jane Gardam	£7.99

The prices shown above are correct at time of going to press. However, the publishers reserve the right to increase prices on covers from those previously advertised, without further notice.

————————— 〈 ABACUS 〉 —————————

Please allow for postage and packing: **Free UK delivery.**
Europe: add 25% of retail price; Rest of World: 45% of retail price.

To order any of the above or any other Abacus titles, please call our credit card orderline or fill in this coupon and send/fax it to:

Abacus, PO Box 121, Kettering, Northants NN14 4ZQ
Fax: 01832 733076   Tel: 01832 737526
Email: aspenhouse@FSBDial.co.uk

☐ I enclose a UK bank cheque made payable to Abacus for £ . . . .
☐ Please charge £ . . . . . . to my Visa/Delta/Maestro

Expiry Date ☐☐☐☐   Maestro Issue No. ☐☐

NAME (BLOCK LETTERS please) . . . .

ADDRESS . . . .

. . . .

. . . .

Postcode . . . . Telephone . . . .

Signature . . . .

Please allow 28 days for delivery within the UK. Offer subject to price and availability.